DAUGHTER-IN-LAW
FROM HELL

LEIGH WILLIAMS

ISBN 978-1-64468-157-2 (Paperback)
ISBN 978-1-64468-158-9 (Digital)

Covenant Books, Inc.
11661 Hwy 707
Murrells Inlet, SC 29576
www.covenantbooks.com

Dedicated to my granddaughter that was emotionally abused. A beautiful little girl with joy and happiness bubbling inside of her until it was squelched by a domineering mother. Her spirit was killed. She rebelled.

Acknowledgements: Thanks to Cathy Lefsky, Martha Bebb, Penny Gell and Kristal Delp for all their help and encouragement. Thanks to Rich Gell for the cover.

Contents

Who Killed Emil

The murder of Emil Paul Russo dominated the front page of the Vindicator newspaper. The night he died he was consumed in thought and completely oblivious to the danger that awaited him. Little did he realize his wife had learned of his affair. She immediately canceled his purchase of the fabulous house he was buying for his mistress.

It was Gloria Russo's inheritance that had funded Emil's four '5-star' restaurants. Anger had boiled up inside of her. She was determined to put an end to her husband's womanizing, one way or another. No longer could she tolerate being betrayed and used.

Emil met Erika Keppel at the Black Diamond Bar two years earlier. Being a very private man, he insisted his lover always sat on the opposite end of the bar. This was to avoid other patrons from making the connection. Erika was forced to acquiesce to his every whim. She had worked hard to persuade him to buy her the mansion. What mattered to her was the life of luxury he could offer. When she learned her new home was canceled she became irate. Bitterness plunged her emotions into an abyss of rage. Her dreams were dashed.

Now Emil Russo had two scorned women out for revenge. Just after midnight, he left the neighborhood bar alone. Walking to his luxury townhouse, his mind was on tomorrow's business luncheon. Seven local executives had reserved the conference room at one of Russo's establishments. As he stepped off the curb to cross South Avenue, two shots rang out. Authorities were confounded. Who shot Mr. Russo in the head? Did Mrs. Russo get the job done? Or did Erika do her a favor?

Nancy, Erika's close friend and roommate, encouraged her to relocate even though Emil's lover couldn't be identified. Knowing neither one can afford the rent alone, they already owe for the past two months, they decided it was time to move on. At one point, Nancy tried to find out Erika's secret, "I'm curious, was it you or his wife who killed Emil?" Erika gave no response; she just raised her brows and slightly smiled.

Erika On the Run

Erika and her best friend, her only friend, Nancy Farcus, are texting as they depart the city where they had wreaked havoc. If there are such things as soul mates, Nancy is Erika's, a God hater with seemingly no conscience, and if possible, more of a sociopath than Erika. The pair had been involved in questionable schemes and had made quite a name for themselves in the city they are leaving behind. Fearing the law may be getting close, they decide to leave town in two different directions. One will head to the airport while the other will take the interstate north.

Erika is packed and rushing to make an appointment in Mooresville, North Carolina. She needs a new start. She's happy to leave her messy past behind her in Columbia, South Carolina. Her gray 2009 Nissan Rogue is flying north on Interstate 77 with the red check engine light on. Screw it, nothing is going to keep her from getting there by noon. Piled high in the back are all her belongings: a favorite leopard pillow rests on top of purses, shoes, sports outfits, sexy dresses, CD's, a laptop and a pink hairdryer. All unorganized, just like her life.

Erika, at 5'8", is a tall, slender and beautiful forty-year-old with a vibrant and fun-loving personality. Her large hazel eyes, with flecks of gold, flash when she speaks. Professionally whitened teeth make her smile even more dazzling. Dressed for the trip in worn blue-jean cutoffs and a comfortable white T-shirt, she loosens her ponytail to free her auburn hair.

It's a warm June morning. The driver's window is down, allowing her shiny hair to blow in the wind. The CD is playing "Born Free." She remembers singing this song as a young girl with her aunt, the black sheep of her mother's family. She was a free spirit and Erika's role model. She wanted to emulate her aunt and live her life free, without boundaries or any moral code. Life was too short not to go after what she wanted at any cost. This is part of her sociopathic roots. She sings along, feeling free from her past. Her only regret was losing that spectacular home Emil was buying for her. His death was no big deal. He was just another man with money.

The canceled estate has seven bedrooms. The master suite overlooks the seventh green of the Dover Country Club. The joy of having her morning coffee on that flagstone terrace is now gone. Gathering her thoughts, she feels sure there will be other fabulous homes in North Carolina. She feels confident there will be one for her.

Headed north, she must forget that house and be happy she's free. The clouds look especially peaceful today. Traffic is light, so speeding is a cinch.

Nancy, also traveling today, is getting ready to leave for the airport. She is an average looking woman, 5'4" with brown eyes and brown hair, not someone who would stand out in a crowd. A bitter divorce has left her with nothing except years of pent up anger. There have been months of unpaid bills. She has given up finding a job in Columbia, her hometown. She noticed a rare opportunity on the Internet. Nancy needs income, so when that offer came in from Albany, New York, she grabbed it. Knowing that a high tax state may make it a wash, she decides to take a chance anyway. She's desperate.

"Hey sis," Erika texts.

"Miss you." Nancy texts back. "I'm leaving for Albany shortly, make sure you're okay".

"I'm fine, better than fine. I need a new start and I'm getting it. Wish you could have come with me."

"We all have to eat."

"True," echoes Erika, "But when you freeze your butt off this winter in Albany, think about moving down south. Everyone needs a partner in crime."

Nancy laughs to herself and texts, "Bye, talk to you soon."

Erika, feeling relaxed, continues her drive to Mooresville. The further she gets from Columbia, the safer she feels. Three hours later her confidence has vanished as she sees blue flashing lights in her rearview mirror. Traveling twenty-two miles over the speed limit, she's nervous. She remembers the six-pack of Bud Lite behind the driver's seat and the two empties on the floor. This could be trouble. Her heart is in her throat. She sees the Gilead exit and guns it up the ramp. There's a break in traffic. Making an illegal turn, she speeds down the opposite ramp right back onto 77 north.

"Don't let me down now car!" Erika yells.

The state patrol is racing to close in on her. He takes the Gilead exit but the gray Nissan is nowhere in sight. He's furious!

Erika's heart is pounding. Is it my speeding? Am I a murder suspect? She keeps watch on her rearview mirror. No blue lights, what a relief. She takes a deep breath to relax, laughs, and then dials up Heidi Bishop.

The call goes to voicemail. "This is Erika, just passed the Gilead exit, be there soon. My interview is at one o'clock at the hospital. I have 451 Palm Tree Lane programmed in my GPS."

It's been twenty years since Erika and Heidi graduated from Tulane University. Although they weren't close friends in college, they were both in the Alpha Delta Sorority. The Alpha Deltas were the hottest things on campus. Heidi took her classes seriously and graduated with honors. Erika was one of the party girls on campus...keggers and staying out late was the norm for her. They had maintained some residual contact through social media.

Heidi is having major reservations about inviting Erika to share her rental, but hadn't come up with any other options. If Erika was still the wild girl she had been in college, there would be some major issues right around the corner. She hoped that Erika had grown up a bit in the past two decades. She would just have to wait and see. Erika sounded like she needed a change of scenery and perhaps Heidi can help her. She is that kind of person, always ready to sacrifice whatever she can to lend a helping hand. Heidi is a straight shooter and honest. Erika, however, had always been careless and reckless, living on the edge.

Twelve miles later she spots Exit 36 to Mooresville. Her engine needle is still on hot, but so far so good. After a few blocks and turns, the GPS guides the Nissan to Palm Tree Lane, a lovely tree-lined street. There are quaint little cottages behind white picket fences on both sides of the street. Real southern charm with large porches dressed for summer, window boxes bursting with flowers, some with sweet potato vines drooping over the sides. Neighbors are walking their dogs. Two little girls are playing with their dolls on a porch swing. It's an all-American neighborhood. Many of the homes have "Ole Glory" mounted on the porch posts. Checking house numbers along the way, she spots 451 painted in white on a black mailbox. A white arbor in the backyard is surrounded by lush green ivy that has spread over the stone wall in front of it. The arbor can be seen from the street, giving a nostalgic feeling to the picturesque cottage. This is the exact type of neighborhood she expected Heidi to be living in, all proper and pristine.

When Erika pulls into the drive, she jumps out and stretches. It's been a long ride. Heidi runs out to welcome her, they share a quick hug. Erika notices her tailored, khaki jumpsuit with brown leather trim. "Wow, that's a sharp outfit!" Heidi is prettier now than when she was in college. "It is so good to see you."

"Thanks, Erika. How was the drive?"

"It was smooth, not much traffic. Can you believe we're going to be roommates? I've always wanted to live in North Carolina." She never mentions the state patrol chase, always trying to protect her image. "You look fabulous Heidi! Your hair is blonder and shorter."

Heidi returns the compliment, "You're still gorgeous."

Erika asks, "How did you find this adorable cottage to rent?"

"The landlords are on an extended mission trip."

Erika has a puzzled look on her face, "Our landlords are missionaries? That's crazy, I gave up on religion years ago. I don't believe any of that God stuff." Heidi pretends to ignore her comments. Erika quietly remarks, "I heard Andy died of a sudden heart attack two years ago, I'm so sorry."

"My husband was studying for the ministry when he died. Andy became a true believer. As a result of his witness, I gave my life to Christ."

"Are you serious? You're a Christian? I try to avoid them. Oh great, I will be living with one. You won't be preaching to me will you?" This arrangement makes Erika feel anxious.

Heidi's beginning to believe that her earlier apprehensions are becoming reality. It's apparent the two have major differences.

She directs the conversation back to Erika, "Whatever happened to you and Brian? Everyone at Tulane felt sure you two would be married."

"Brian's mother was totally against me. Guess I was too strong and independent for her son. He was the love of my life and she destroyed our relationship. I haven't been able to forgive her." Erika explains, "When I think of his mother, anger wells up inside of me. After twenty years I should be over it, but I'm not. I still love Brian and I still hate his mother!"

Wanting to change the subject, Heidi tells her, "Erika, as beautiful as you are, I'm sure you'll capture someone's heart."

"Thanks for the compliment. I would love to meet a man with money. Ever since I was a little girl I've dreamed of living in a big beautiful house. I want a mansion!" The loss of the spectacular estate from Emil flashes in her mind; it was a colossal disappointment.

"Erika, after your job interview, I'll show you around the cottage and treat you to a late lunch. Before you leave, check out our front porch. It's like an extra room and it's always in the shade because of this wonderful tree.

Erika notices, "I like the cobalt rug and the white wicker furniture." She says sarcastically, "What's with the American flag? I'm not fond of the flag. The flag, the constitution, and the Bible need to be discarded or revised. They are long overdue. We are living in different times, things change."

A shocked look comes over Heidi's face...disbelief. She has a hard time learning that Erika is against the very values she holds dear: the flag, the Bible, and the constitution. Heidi begins to feel a wave of nausea, but decides not to dwell on their differences. The commitment to share rent with Erika has been made. Going back on her word isn't something Heidi would consider.

Erika remarks, "I told my friend, Nancy, I'll be living in a southern cottage. She wants to hear all about it. They have always been intriguing to her. I'm expecting it to be very charming and I'm anxious to see the inside. First, I better change clothes and get to the hospital. May I change in your bathroom? I should be back soon. The ICU coordinator is expecting me."

An hour later, Erika is home from the hospital. She's all smiles when she walks through the door. Heidi knows it's good news. She is anxious to hear how her interview went. They share high-fives. "I start in three days."

Heidi says, "I'm so happy for you."

"Thanks Heidi, for allowing me to share your home. Maybe I'll meet the man of my dreams in Mooresville."

Next they tour the cottage. She's impressed and surprised to see how nice it is. "This place is so unique!" Heidi offers her the larger bedroom. It has a good size TV, in a French armoire, nestled between the two windows. The dark wood ceiling fan will be great for warm Carolina nights. Light grey walls show off the white, weathered headboard. On each side of the bed are heavy oak cabinets with stately matching lamps. A pair of French white-washed chairs, upholstered in cream linen, flank a table made of dark oak. Two horse paintings take their place on the wall over the table. Best of all, in the back, it has its own bathroom. Erika sees the beautiful glass shower and generously sized soaking tub, "This is incredible." The large walk-in closet will soon be filled with all her belongings. "This is very kind of you, Heidi.

Are you okay with the two small bedrooms up front and the hall bath?"

"No problem. I want you to have the master suite," she tells Erika, "I'm content with that. I'll use one small bedroom for a sitting room. It has a large bookcase so I can stack all of my books in it." Erika feels she deserves the master suite and doesn't want bookcases. She has no books, reading bores her.

Suddenly Erika's cell phone rings. She excuses herself to take the call. Nancy Farcus is on the line and Erika is upset because she called. Abruptly, she reminds her friend not to call again. She wants to converse with Nancy in private and on her own terms.

Nancy explains, "I was concerned and wanted to know you arrived safely. Sorry I upset you."

Erika doesn't bother to ask how her trip to Albany went. She tells her friend, "Please let me call you, but as long as you're on the line, don't hang up. I have a real shocker to tell you, I'm rooming with a born-again Christian. I can't believe it! You've always warned me about those people. They're weird. What are the odds of this happening? Why me? I do not want someone judging everything I do. She says she won't but we'll see. I'm not very comfortable with it. Christians seem to think they are the only ones that have it right."

Nancy insists, "Don't get caught up in that religious craziness. You're great the way you are!"

Erika laughs, "Don't worry, I'm not that needy. Do you want to hear about the cottage?"

Nancy replies, "I've been waiting."

Erika tells her, "It's like a rustic cabin. There's a fishing pole mounted over the desk. A big chunk of birch is the base of a lamp. The only rug on the dark hardwood floors is a brown-and-white cowhide; a canvas of a white bull proudly sits on top of the mantle. Old wooden tools, antlers, and 3-D animal heads enhance the walls. The whole place is done in neutrals. The outside looks like a southern cottage, but the inside looks more like a mountain cabin. I'll text you pictures later. You really need a visual to appreciate the place. I have to hang up now, Heidi is taking me to an Italian restaurant for lunch. We are meeting a friend of hers from church, a Marty Scott or something. I know what you're thinking, don't worry. I'm not going to any church, not me. Nancy, you know we have both discussed how phony church people can be. It's not for me. Put your mind at rest, we made a pact, didn't we? No God! I'll call you later, Heidi is waiting for me." Erika hangs up, not even waiting for a response.

They unload Erika's things from the car. Erika apologizes, "The car needs to be swept out."

Heidi is unconcerned about it. "That can wait, let's head to the restaurant. Aren't you hungry? I don't want to keep Marty waiting. You drive, I'll tell you the directions." They climb into the Nissan. Heidi reminds her, "Buckle your seatbelt, they're very strict around here." Erika tells her that the car has been overheating. Heidi lets her know about a place where she can get her car serviced on Monday.

"It can wait," Erika replied.

"You'll like Marty, she has a great sense of humor. She's the first one that welcomed me when I moved here and we've been friends ever since. She's close to our age, early forties. She introduced me to many wonderful people. Marty is a great friend."

Erika backs out of the driveway. "Wow!" Heidi speaks out, "You just missed our mailbox." Soon they're headed up Market Street. Heidi is tense, Erika's driving way too fast. She tells her the speed limit, but Erika pretends not to hear. They come to a stop sign, she is unable to stop and they zoom right through it. Heidi is shocked and yells, "What are you doing? That was a stop sign!" A loud screeching sound is heard as a blue car slams on its brakes, then a loud bang. Black skid marks are left on the pavement. An unexpected driver in a red jeep smashes into the rear end of the blue car. Busted headlights scatter broken pieces of glass on the street.

Erika doesn't stop. Heidi is angry and disgusted. She didn't expect such recklessness and total disregard for others. She takes a deep breath and speaks out. "What if someone was injured? That was a hit-and-run! You have to go back!"

Erika quickly retorts, "I didn't hit anyone. It won't do any good to go back; besides, I'm behind on my auto insurance. I can't take a chance." Heidi quietly prays for the victims of the crash and wonders if any bystanders got Erika's license plate number.

Heidi realizes Erika hasn't changed. She was always wild and unconcerned about the rules. She worries that Erika's behavior might reflect upon her good reputation in the community. She was recently hired as a pharmacist at a local drug store. They both have responsible jobs with Erika now a nurse at the regional hospital.

She inhales deeply, letting her breath out slowly. How is she going to deal with this crazy woman? It will take prayer and patience. Just thinking about it is exasperating enough.

Lunch With Marty

Continuing up Market Street, they come to Little Italy on the right. Erika is impressed with the Italian architecture. The sun is shining on the rusty colored tiled roof. The arches stand out on the structure. Erika's never been to Italy but imagines it must look like this.

Some of the lunch crowd has left, parking is easy. As they walk toward the black awning-covered entrance, two handsome businessmen in tailored suits are leaving. They are Mark Larson and John Barringer. John catches Erika's attention. He's tall, dark and handsome. His dark brown hair is neatly combed. They call out, "Hi, Heidi!"

Mark says, "See you Sunday. We have a meeting, have to run."

The men climb into a shiny black Mercedes and drive away. Erika is very impressed. She wonders how she can gracefully ask Heidi to introduce her to them. Why did the one say, "See you Sunday?" Erika assumes they go to the same church.

The two women enter the restaurant, Erika finds it very charming. Rough hand-hewn beams brace the ceiling. White stucco walls are yellowed with age. Several round tables with antique bentwood chairs fill the large room. Each table, covered with a red and white checkered tablecloth, has a Chianti wine bottle for a candle-holder. Adding to the charm, globs of wax have been built up over time on each bottle. Lit candles flicker as a slow-moving ceiling fan stirs the air. One can almost feel they're in Italy. A short chubby Italian man with a mustache strolls among the guests playing his violin. The smell of spaghetti whets their appetite. A heavyset host-ess leads them to a table. "Your server will be with you shortly." Heidi suggests the antipasto salad served with fresh warm Italian bread. That sounds great to Erika.

Just then, Marty walks in. She tells Erika how anxious she's been to meet her. "Welcome to North Carolina, Erika. You'll love our town. People are so friendly, and the weather is great."

Heidi says, "I've ordered our usual, Marty."

Erika hears Heidi mention that she'll say grace. Just before heads are bowed, Erika has an excuse to run to the restroom. Soon she's back and their salads are served.

They enjoy lunch and share small talk. The waiter hears their soft giggles as they enjoy each other's com-pany. Erika is nervous; she folds and refolds her large paper napkin.

She can't wait any longer, "I'm curious Heidi, are the two good-looking men married?"

Marty has a puzzled look on her face, "What men?"

Heidi clarifies, "Mark and John were leaving as we walked in. No Erika, they're single, but they aren't your type. They tag-team the adult Bible study at Lakeside Chapel."

Marty adds, "I teach Kid Zone there."

Heidi replies, "You are welcome to come to church with us."

Erika hesitates, but then says, "I'd feel weird; I've put God out of my life. He has never done anything for me, besides nobody wants to give up everything that is fun for religion. God has too many do's and don'ts."

Heidi answers, "That is a better reason to come. You'll see that we all have a great time. We would love for you to join us."

How would she meet Heidi's handsome friends if she doesn't go to their church? She had made a pact with Nancy Farcus, no religion. But this was not about going to church. Nancy would understand. She lets them know that she will go. Marty and Heidi are happy to hear it.

After a wonderful lunch, Marty leaves for her exercise class at the Y. She's been trying to drop fifteen pounds. Heidi and Erika head for the parking lot. She thanks Heidi for lunch then asks, "Your friends, is John the taller one?"

"Yes, John is taller than Mark."

Back in the Nissan, Erika reminds Heidi, "All of my clothes are too sexy to wear to church. Could we go shopping?" Heidi decides to give Erika a loan until she starts work.

Heidi takes her to a neat little boutique downtown. Searching rack after rack for conservative clothes in size 6, they gather up an armful of choices and head for the dressing room. The navy-and-white outfit looks matronly.

Erika clowns in front of the mirror, dramatizing how bad it looks as they both giggle.

Erika says, "Please hand me the red dress."

Heidi thinks this one is perfect. "It will go well with your hair."

Erika remarks, "What about the white dress? Is the neckline too low for church?"

Heidi says, "No, the neck is fine. You look fantastic in white; it shows off your suntan. Great choices, get both of them."

They go to the front and checkout. An older lady in her middle seventies is at the cash register. She comments; "Oh girls, I remember when I would buy sleeveless dresses like these. Enjoy your youth, the years go by fast."

Erika asks Heidi, "Do you mind stopping at a Christian bookstore? I will need a Bible to look the part."

Heidi's eager to help her out and hopes she'll read it. It's a short drive to 'Redeemed', the Christian bookstore in a small plaza next to a barbershop. Erika parks as close as she can. They walk to the store; Heidi holds the glass door open for Erika. It's the first time she's been in a religious store and is overwhelmed with all the choices. She depends on the store clerk for help. The clerk encourages Erika to buy an ICR Bible because it has solid footnotes. "It's a great learning tool." The clerk doesn't realize her customer has no interest in studying the book she's buying. Politely, Erika thanks her for the help and makes the purchase. Back in the car she recklessly throws her new purchase in the backseat. This upsets Heidi, she hates seeing God's word handled with such irreverence. Heidi bites her tongue as she realizes that she is going to have to pick her battles with Erika.

As they drive away, Heidi informs Erika, "The next Bible I buy will be that one. God has used Dr. Henry Morris to explain verses. He's a creationist."

Erika asks, "What does that mean?"

"He believes God created everything for His glory. God speaks to us through his written word. How we live reflects what we believe."

Erika is fidgeting with her hair and looking out the window, making it obvious to Heidi that she's heard enough. "That means nothing to me. I'm totally disconnected from God and am just fine with it. I don't believe religion is a topic that should be discussed."

Hearing Erika's total disregard for God is very disheartening for Heidi. It's difficult for her to be silent concerning her faith. She loves to talk about God, His attributes, and His absolute sovereignty. She didn't get very far with Erika, but maybe she will hear the truth in church and be changed by it. Right now, Erika wants no part of God.

Before heading back home, Erika stops at a kiosk to rent a movie. After selecting an Oscar-winning love story, they're soon relaxing at the cottage.

Heidi prepares pita bread stuffed with cucumber slices, pepper jack cheese, and hummus to enjoy as they watch the movie. All evening Erika has a hard time concentrating on the story. She is anticipating what it will be like to meet John tomorrow. What should she wear?

Should she pretend to be quiet and shy? Maybe he'll be more attracted to her if she comes off happy and fun. She has a lot of experience playing a variety of personalities, but a Christian, this one will be new for her. All these thoughts go through her mind.

The movie is over. Heidi remarks, "What a happy ending, I love the way it turned out." Erika doesn't comment since she wasn't concentrating on the story. Heidi ignores it and tells her, "Erika, I'm going to put our dishes in the sink and go to bed. Good night, see you in the morning. Try to be ready by 8:15."

Erika responds, "Good night Heidi," and goes to her room. Turning on some soft romantic music to fall to sleep by, she dreams of a positive encounter with John.

Sunday Morning

Eight hours later the sun is up; it's time to get ready for church. Erika is sure she'll make a great impression with John. All morning her mind has been on dating him. In Erika's mind, they are already a couple. After a quick shower, she goes to the kitchen for a cup of hot tea. Piling globs of orange marmalade on a croissant, she checks the time. It's getting late, she better get a move on. Choosing the red dress, she then slips into her black strappy shoes. Bright red lipstick may look too worldly; she goes for a softer color. Wanting to appear Christian, she decides against the large drop earrings, she puts on smaller gold ones.

It's now twenty-five after and Heidi is ready to leave. "Let's go, Erika. We want to get there early. They have a social time with coffee and pastries. It's a chance to make new acquaintances."

Erika dabs on Jessica McClintock perfume behind each ear before rushing out the door.

Heidi comments on Erika's fabulous perfume, "You smell good, like lilies in the spring."

Erika pulls the visor down to double-check her hair. Next, she opens her purse to make sure she put tissue and gum in the side pockets.

She is very excited that she's going to meet John! Men have always been attracted to her flirty little ways. This should be easy, she feels confident about herself. She compliments Heidi, "You look fabulous this morning."

Heidi's wearing a powder blue suit; the silver buttons match her silver jewelry. To prevent a scary ride, Heidi makes sure she's driving today. She remembers Erika's heavy foot on the gas pedal and the crash she caused. It appears that Erika's license plate number was not reported as there have been no repercussions from the wreck.

They're buckled in her light-yellow VW Beetle. The license plate is custom and reads 'Lemon Pie'. Driving through a high-end neighborhood, Erika is impressed. They pass several amazing estates before coming to the church. Erika comments, "I will live in a mansion like one of these someday." Heidi ignores the remark.

They arrive at the park-like setting. Brick posts, partially hidden by the deep blue hydrangeas at the entrance, welcome each one attending. It is a beautiful traditional red-brick church. The front entry is flanked with eight tall white pillars. Symmetrical stained-glass windows show off the heavy varnished oak doors. The steeple is high and demanding as it rises skyward. On the very top is a cross pointing to the heavens.

Erika feels intimidated. Heidi looks for a parking space. They park near the door next to a red convertible. Erika admires the shiny red Camaro; the top is down showing off the clean white leather seats. It's very impressive. Heidi notices and tells Erika the Camaro belongs to Jennifer Davis and that she would probably get to meet her. She adds that Jennifer will be the one with the gorgeous red hair.

There are several other cars in the parking lot. More cars are waiting on the main road, ready to turn in. Erika can't understand why so many people are interested in attending church. To her it was always boring.

The two women briskly walk up the wide brick steps. A young boy in his teens smiles as he opens the heavy church door for them. Inside, a short white haired usher welcomes them. Erika questions, "Why is he wearing a grey and maroon plaid jacket from the 1960's?

She whispers, "He's a little strange isn't he?"

Heidi clears it up. "No, that's Marvin Goldberg, he's a good guy. I've been told that he's been attending here for a long time. His wife died a few years ago."

Erika thinks about his name, "Isn't he Jewish?"

Heidi explains, "Marvin is a Messianic Jew. He's come full circle and now knows that Jesus is the Jewish Messiah. There are a lot of prophecies in the Old Testament about Jesus and Isaiah 53 is one of them. It was written 722 years before Christ died on the cross."

Erika asks, "Why does he believe the Bible?"

Heidi explains, "Marvin will tell you that it's because of God's grace and that the Bible proves itself in all the fulfilled prophecies. Marvin loves to talk about the prophecy concerning Israel. God scattered the Jews among the nations because of their unbelief and blinded them from the truth, Amos 8:11–12. God promised to one day restore their land, Amos 9:15. Approximately four thousand years later,

God put President Truman in office at the right time. Daniel 2:21. God removes Kings and sets up kings [and presidents]. All of Washington was against signing the renewed land to Israel, but Truman knew his Bible. He knew God's prophecy. He prayed for the right answer. So on May 14, 1948, it was official, Israel became a nation. Erika, all of God's prophecies come true in His time. His timing is perfect. Isaiah 66:8 says, 'Shall a nation be born at once?'"

Erika says, "Heidi, you really believe it was God's doing, don't you? It sounds pretty far-fetched to me. I can't accept that. It must have been a coincidence, a freaky coincidence."

Heidi tells her, "The Bible says in Acts 28:24, some believe, some believe not. One of my favorite verses is John 10:27–28; where Jesus said, "My sheep hear My voice, I know them and they follow Me. I give eternal life to them and they will never perish. No one is able to snatch them out of My hand."

Erika has heard enough. She flippantly rolls her eyes and tosses her head hoping that's all she'll have to endure.

They head to Bible study. Rushing down the hall, Heidi's shoe comes off. She snickers softly as she stops to put it back on then continues to hurry to class.

Heidi has always been the prettiest woman there. Now, all heads turn when gorgeous Erika walks in. Some of the women are intimidated, others don't seem to be bothered. All the men take a second look but Erika pretends not to notice. Mark walks over to meet and welcome Heidi's friend.

Heidi tells him, "I want you to meet Erika Keppel. She is sharing my rented cottage with me. We went to college together in New Orleans. I can't believe how long it's been since we graduated. Seems like only a couple of years ago."

Mark tells Erika, "You picked a good person to team up with. We think a lot of Heidi."

Erika smiles agreeing warmly, "She's a good person. I'm curious, what do you contribute to the fact that so many attend this Bible study? There must be sixty-five people here."

Marks answers, "We are growing. People want to fill the hole in their hearts. They try to fill their emptiness with material things, drugs, pleasures, relationships, and many more things but only Jesus Christ can fill that void. That is how God wired us when He created us. Christ alone is the answer."

Erika is at a loss for words. Heidi is afraid of what Erika might say, so she jumps in, "Let's get some coffee. Do you want to join us, Mark?"

As they finish their coffee, he notices Erika is checking out the group. She spots John across the room; he's wearing a beige golf shirt. Being 6'5", he stands out in the crowd. He's probably the most handsome man she has ever seen. She wonders how she can be in love with a man she has never met. She must catch his eye; the best option is to have Mark walk over with her. Mark is okay with it.

Suddenly Erika spots a tall redhead in a navy-blue dress over by the window glaring at her. It is Jennifer Davis. Erika acts unconcerned but she can almost feel the woman's green eyes piercing through her. The woman puts on her black rim glasses to get a better look at Erika. She is checking out the competition. Mark walks up to John, "Please meet Erika, she's Heidi's friend. She just moved here from Columbia, South Carolina. She and Heidi are roommates."

John introduces himself, "Very glad you came today, welcome."

Jennifer sees gorgeous Erika as someone John could become interested in. She immediately maneuvers her way over. A flash of jealousy comes over her face. Erika suddenly recognizes her. "Didn't I see you at the hospital? It was ICU, right? I'm going to be working there too." Jennifer is also a critical care R.N.

Jennifer coldly responds, "You might have," and turns away from Erika. This sends Erika a clear message that John is hers and she wants no competition. Jennifer reminds John that she needs to discuss her baptism with him, it's coming up soon. John is put on the spot. He's been dating Jennifer and doesn't want to hurt her feelings. On the other hand, he wants to be friendly to newcomers. It is very awkward.

John tells Erika, "It's nice meeting you. Please excuse me." Erika feels snubbed. It doesn't take much to offend her. She is hurt and humiliated. In her mind John was going to be swept off his feet.

Mark notices that Erika isn't very happy. He tells her, "Jennifer has been trying to be John's significant other for some time. They have been dating for a few months." Erika is feeling left out. She wants to avenge Jennifer for manipulating John's time.

Rejection

Erika can't take rejection and she just got a big dose of it. It was Jennifer's fault that she didn't get to spend more time with John. She is determined that that won't happen again.

Twenty minutes later, Mark and John go to the front of the group to prepare to teach. Mark announces, "A question and answer session will follow."

Class begins. Heidi and Erika sit in the second row. Heidi is following the lesson in her Bible. Erika keeps her attention on John, admiring his good looks. It is a double whammy when John doesn't even glance her way as he teaches. She is not accustomed to this lack of attention from a man. When class is over, she will try again to get him to notice her.

The study is on Colossians 1:16–17. After the study, Heidi tells Mark what a good job he and John did. "You cleared up some things for me."

John walks over to talk to Jennifer again. Erika is really upset now! She can't believe this. She bought two new dresses and a Bible she didn't want and now she gets the shaft a third time. She is furious, worse yet, she owes Heidi $150.00.

Walking to the parking lot, Heidi notices the disgusted look on Erika's face. Her lips are drawn tight and she's breathing heavily. Heidi hopes she'll lighten up as they climb into the car. On the way home, it's very icy in the yellow Volkswagen Beetle.

Heidi asks Erika, "Would you like to stop for brunch? I know a nice little restaurant."

The answer comes back sharp and quick. "No thanks." Heidi is taken back by her rudeness. She has no idea Erika was seriously planning on John falling all over her. Heidi just knows Erika is really upset.

Mark has invited Heidi to go to a concert. She wants to share her good news with Erika to try and connect with her but sees it is not a good time. Mark is 6'1" with brown hair, slightly receding at the temples. There's something about Mark that reminds her of Andy. She's interested in him but isn't one to let it show. Mark has never been married, only engaged once to a beautiful blonde dental assistant. She broke up with him to be with the owner of the largest car dealership in the Tri-State. It left him heartbroken, but he is now ready for a new relationship.

An Evil Plan

Back at their cottage, Erika is still in one of her ugly moods. No other words have been spoken. She goes into her room and slams the door. Grabbing her phone, she flops down on the side of the bed. Kicking off her shoes, she calls someone who will listen, Nancy.

As soon as she hears Nancy's voice, her mood lightens. "I met this tall, handsome guy this morning in church. I couldn't take my eyes off of him."

Nancy can't believe what she's hearing. "Let me sit down, you went to church? Are you serious? Hold on, I have to get a grip on this. Did you forget our pact? No religion."

Erika tries to settle her down. There's a lengthy silence. "I've met the man I'm going to marry. I did go to church; it had nothing to do with God. I just wanted to meet this guy. I will treat him better than the ones in Columbia. I learned what not to do from those relationships. This will be different, trust me, I know what I'm doing. We will be married. There are only three problems: One, he barely knows I exist. Two, he is a Christian. Three, he has his eye on another woman." Three strikes should mean she's out, but not Erika. She's in it to win it!

"Are you out of your mind? I think you've lost it," her friend tells her.

Erika says, "You know I can fake being a Christian. I need a way to get rid of the other woman. Her name is Jennifer Davis. She thinks she is so smart driving to Bible study in her flashy red convertible. She must be removed from the picture, I don't want the competition. How can I make it happen? Help me out, you always have an answer."

"Did I hear you say she drives a convertible? I'm sure the top is down at times. Calm down Erika. Did you forget about the water bottle? You did it before and it worked, you know just how to place it."

"Thanks, Nancy, I forgot all about that. Why didn't I think of this? You always come through for me."

Her evil friend reminds her, "You will have to be a sweet, loving person to everyone you come in contact with. No one will ever suspect such a good person. Besides that, you don't even know this woman, you just met her. I want you to let me know if it works. The results are important to me, I keep score, remember? Do you realize you are asking me to help you marry a Christian? What won't I do for you?"

Erika gets the picture; she remembers how well the bottle worked in Columbia. Evil overtakes her as she plans it all out in her mind. No one will know except Nancy. With Jennifer gone, she will be there to win John over. No man has ever been able to resist her when she pours on her charms. It will take time and patience

because John is no ordinary man. He's a real catch, successful, good-looking and single!

Selecting the right day is next, the sooner the better.
She just wants to get the job done. The Nissan has been
repaired. It's a relief to see the red check light off.

Guilt Free

A week later, Erika has had time to contemplate how she will accomplish the job. Overwhelmed with urgency, she checks the hospital schedule. It looks like the best time for her plan to work will be in two days. Erika starts her shift at 3:00 pm. She'll be on her way to work when Jennifer will be finishing her shift. A perfect opportunity to get rid of the competition.

Finally, the day arrives. Today is the day. As she drives to the hospital she puts in a CD of heavy metal. The volume is up to drown out her thoughts. Two more red lights and she'll be there.

Jennifer has the top down on her convertible on sunny days and parks in the same place every time she goes to work. Erika pulls into the hospital parking lot. She sees Jennifer's car, the top is down and the coast is clear. Walking over, she places the plastic water bottle just right. It's easy for Erika; nothing stands in the way once she decides what she wants. Glancing around to make certain no one saw her, she walks along the black iron fence. Erika feels hidden; four large pine trees conceal her. Entering the front hospital doors, she takes the elevator to the fourth floor. Jennifer is just clocking out for the day. They do not make eye contact, Erika wants to avoid her. She doesn't feel anything is wrong if it's done for a good reason. She always gets what she wants. Why should another woman stand in her way?

Erika soon gets busy in ICU and doesn't have time to think about what she did. Eight hours later, she finishes up and clocks out. Down the elevator she heads for the exit, happy the main hall is empty. Out on the sidewalk, with the fresh breeze in her face, she feels relieved. She tosses her used gum in the neatly trimmed hedge and walks along the black iron fence. Back to her Nissan, she climbs in and speeds away.

Erika is excited to go home and wait for the news about Jennifer to come in. Soon she's back at the cottage enjoying a ham sandwich and a cold glass of beer. When Heidi gets home; she tosses the mail on the desk. The smell of beer is evident; she's concerned about Erika's excessive alcohol intake but says nothing.

Heidi comments, "Looks like we got a lot of junk mail. Oh, there are two utility bills in the pile. I'll take care of them."

Guilt-free, Erika reminds her, "There is ham and Swiss cheese in the fridge." It's easy for her to compartmentalize her deeds. A silly quote comes to Erika's mind, "remove God and Satan will fill the vacuum." It goes along with the statement Mark made in church about the hole in people's hearts. It's so ridiculous! There's no such thing as Satan. With that thought, she goes to the kitchen for another beer.

Later that evening, Heidi and Erika are both enjoying a buttery bowl of popcorn. Heidi is paying a few bills at the desk. Erika is relaxing in her silky lavender pajamas on the sofa, looking at fashion magazines. All of a sudden the phone rings, it's Mark. Heidi takes the call, "Oh no, that's terrible!" Erika hears the horror in her voice. Heidi says, "I feel terrible. Does John know? Oh, it's hard to believe. Did you say John knew? Erika could barely hear Mark's voice over the phone, "Yes, John is devastated and in shock. Jennifer died instantly." Heidi moves the phone from her ear to tell Erika, "Jennifer Davis was killed in a terrible crash. Do you remember her?"

Erika nods her head yes to let Heidi know she recalls her. She pretends to be stunned and shocked. "How did it happen?" Springing off the sofa, her magazines fall on the floor. Clamping one hand over her mouth in disbelief, she lets out a gasp.

Heidi puts the phone on speaker. Mark says, "The state patrolman said Jennifer was entering 77 South when a big white semi was barreling down the right lane. He said she couldn't stop. There was a plastic water bottle lodged under her brake pedal. It's one of the worst accidents he's ever seen. They could only identify her by her license plate and nurse's badge. That section of 77 is closed. The semi lost control, skidded into the median and turned on its side. The driver wasn't hurt. Traffic will be tied up for hours. I am going over to John's to spend time with him. He is so shaken. The pastor is there now. I'll call you later Heidi, to give you an update."

Erika pretends to be shocked. "How terrible, I feel sick about it." She must be careful to conceal the pride and joy she feels over a job masterfully executed. She jokes to herself; the path to marrying John is now open.

John is taking Jennifer's death very hard. Mark didn't realize he cared so much for her. John was barely over the loss of his wife, Amy, who died of cancer 3 years ago.

Three days later the funeral is set. Heidi and Erika search through their closets for black attire. Heidi decided on a long-tailored skirt with a matching black jacket and a single strand of pearls. Erika chose a black pantsuit with black lace sleeves and a gold necklace.

They pull up and park to enter the grand Victorian funeral home. They enter and a man in a black suit ushers them in and leads them to sign the guestbook. The funeral home is packed, standing room only. The intense smell of roses and the sound of drone organ music are nauseating to Erika. She's been to too many funerals. It's not the sadness that upsets her, but all the silly fanfare when someone dies. It seems needless and ridiculous.

The funeral is painful for all who knew her; everyone has tears in their eyes. Such a terrible accident; loved ones are in disbelief. John is having a hard time knowing that he will never see Jennifer again in this life.

Erika has her eye on John, but he doesn't seem to notice her. After the funeral is over, Erika and Heidi stop to console Jennifer's parents. Mr. and Mrs. Davis have lost their only child. They share a hug as Erika tells them, "I feel your pain."

Before Erika realizes it, three months have passed since Jennifer's death. Erika has been quietly going to work and helping out at Lakeside Chapel. Heidi and Mark went to the concert and have been dating ever since.

John is starting to heal. One evening, he stops at Mark's to watch the Cleveland Indians play the Yankees. During the 7th inning stretch, the conversation turns toward Mark and Heidi. Mark tells John he feels sure he's going to ask Heidi to marry him. John laughs, "You've been looking for Ms. Right your whole life. I believe you just like to look. You can't be serious."

Mark begs to differ with him. "John, you have to get on with your life. What about Erika? She has been so faithful at church. Would you consider going on a double date with Heidi and me?" John thinks about it and then agrees.

"You make the plans on when and where and I'll call Erika. I know that I have to get on with my life. My daughters have suffered enough with their mom gone, they were just becoming close to Jennifer. They need some happiness. You're right Mark; it's time for me to live again."

Erika's Scheme

Erika knew it was only a matter of time before John would call. She was scheduled to work the night they planned, but she decided to call off sick. Nothing would interfere with a date with John Barringer. The ICU nurse believed her when she claimed to be sick.

On Friday evening, they drive to a local pizza shop near the lake. Mark selects a table outside where they can see the water and boats. Heidi feels compelled to warn John about Erika's character flaws but trusts John's good sense and intellect to figure it out for himself. Besides, maybe her prayers will be answered and Erika will give her life to Christ. Even Heidi doesn't realize the capacity of Erika's devious behaviors. If she did they wouldn't even be roommates.

Heidi and Erika select the toppings for the pizza. Mark orders a pitcher of ice-cold Pepsi. Erika would prefer an ice-cold beer, but she doesn't say a thing. On the tray are four frosted mugs, four paper plates, and a stack of white paper napkins. Their conversation is light. John has a great sense of humor, so they all laugh a lot. John and Erika seem to have great chemistry.

"Where do you work, John?"

"Mark and I are both attorneys. We work at my father's firm, Barringer Nelson and Allen. I've heard that you work at the hospital in ICU. Did you work with Jennifer?"

Erika says, "No, she worked a different shift. I felt so bad when I heard what happened to her, heard you took it hard." Lying is easy and natural for her.

John admits, "It was a painful time, I'm healing though."

Erika asks, "How long have you and Mark been friends?"

"We've been friends since Harvard Law School. We were the only Christians in our class. Sometimes it wasn't easy, fearing backlash from unbelieving professors. But we had the Lord and each other for encouragement."

The waiter collects the empty trays. John orders coffee as they relax and get better acquainted. Mark and Heidi decide to walk down by the lake.

John says, "We can't leave until they come back. Did you know I have two sweet young daughters? They are very special, I adore them."

Erika is surprised, "I had no idea, I love kids. Show me pictures. Please tell me all about them."

As John opens his wallet and reveals pictures, he explains, "Their mother died from cancer three years ago, but they are doing okay. Kim is four and she doesn't remember her mom. She loves to play with her dolls. Taylor is six and loves to draw, I save all her drawings, I'll show you one day. Actually I save all of their drawings. I have a hard time throwing anything they create away."

Erika says, "They are adorable, I would love to meet them."

John feels relieved that Erika likes kids. That would have derailed this relationship even before it started. His girls are his priority. "Would you like to join us Sunday afternoon? My daughters and I always set that time aside for our ice cream date."

Erika responds, "I will look forward to that, I'm very excited to meet them." Erika is very proud of herself. She set out to get John interested in her and it's working out just fine. She admits, "I'm honored that you would include me in the ice cream date."

John asks, "Can we pick you up at two o'clock?"

Plans are set; Erika will be on her best behavior. She won't let anything mess this up. She knows exactly how to captivate a man so there's no escape. Soon John won't know what hit him. He will be under her spell! GAME ON!

Beauty is a powerful asset, but it can be dangerous when mixed with deceit and malevolence. Erika has both. Will John see this, or will love be blind?

Erika wants to make a big impression. She goes to a toy department and selects two cute brown and white teddy bears with lime-green polka-dot bows, the perfect size for little girls.

When the doorbell rings Sunday afternoon, John proudly introduces his two beautiful blond daughters dressed in pink and white. They are cuter than she expected, hugs are shared. As Erika gives the bears to Taylor and Kim, she effervesces, "I love your pink shirts and check out those white sandals. You girls are adorable!" She is surprised at how sincere she sounds.

John speaks out, "Did I get the bows in their hair right?"

"Perfect bows for perfect girls, John."

He takes charge. "Let's go, Taylor and Kim are anxious to go for ice cream."

Soon they are sitting outside the ice cream shop under a large blue umbrella. They are licking fast to keep the vanilla cones from dripping. Now Kim is concerned because ice cream has dripped on her white shorts. She painfully stares at the spot.

Taylor speaks up, "Don't worry Kim, Daddy will wash them."

John then reassures her, "That's what washing machines are for, Honey."

Erika is impressed by how he handled that. After the ice cream cones are finished, Erika has a good idea. "Let's play guess what I see."

Erika goes first so they will know how the game is played. They each find an object and the others have to guess what they see. Taylor and Kim love it! When their dad can't figure out what they are looking at, they laugh. John plays along, pretending not to guess the right answer. His daughters snicker when he can't find the items. Erika plays along also. Soon they decide it's time to go; the girls run to the car. It was lots of fun playing the guessing game.

Kim says, "Hurry Daddy."

Back at the cottage, Erika invites them in. She has planned another surprise. "John, help them up on the kitchen bar stools." She has paper and markers all ready to teach them how to draw cartoons. John is impressed as he stands back and watches. He's surprised to see the funny characters they come up with. Erika and the girls have fun laughing at the cartoons. They draw crazy shapes for heads, and then add exaggerated noses and silly looking eyes.

"Erika, you are so good with kids. I'm surprised you didn't choose teaching as a career." A gentle smile comes over her face. She is painfully and patiently doing her best to play the part.

As they are about to leave, Erika comes up with a request. "I would like it if each of you girls would select a cartoon for me. I can tape them on our refrigerator, it will remind me of all the fun we had."

Taylor and Kim have a hard time deciding which cartoon to give up. Finally, they each give Erika one for the fridge. Erika knows how to score points; John is very impressed. His daughters thank Erika as they leave. Wait until Nancy hears the latest!

Nancy Gets a Call

Her guests are gone; she immediately calls Nancy Farcus. "Hi, it's your best friend with an update. I'm making headway with John, but I'll have to deal with his two little brats. He is crazy about his daughters. You know I never liked kids. Imagine competing with 4 and 6 year-olds. They make me so jealous, especially the oldest one, Taylor."

Nancy straightens her out. "You're never happy Erika. If your end goal is to marry this guy, be kind to his daughters. You'll have to be if you're going to pull this off. You know, you never called me to let me know if the water bottle worked."

Erika sharply answers, "It worked, but listen to me Nancy, in my mind it had nothing to do with me. It's over and I will never speak of it again. Do you hear that?" Erika abruptly slams down the phone hurting Nancy's ears. Nancy knows her well, this will pass.

Heidi arrives home, she's anxious to hear how the ice cream date went. Erika explains, "I adore John's little girls. They are so sweet and very polite. He's a great father."

Heidi isn't surprised to hear this; she smiles and nods her head. "They are truly precious; they've been through a lot. Losing their mother was tough enough and they were just beginning to get attached to Jennifer. They deserve to be happy and loved." Heidi is concerned about them. She has a tender spot for John's girls.

Mark and Heidi have been seeing each other for a while and are getting serious. Heidi feels John will be a good influence on Erika. She needs a strong partner.

One day, as they walked to the car, an older gentleman casually asks John, "How's your golf game, John?" Hearing this, Erika realizes he is a golfer. This will work out in her favor. Knowing the Masters is on this weekend, she invites John over.

Game of Golf

Sunday afternoon the doorbell rings, without hesitation she jumps up and opens the door, John is right on time.

"Come in, it's good to see you. John hugs Erika and says, "So often I've thought about the nice day I spent with you and the girls." Glancing at the refrigerator, he sees the cartoons Taylor and Kim drew are still on display. "That is so thoughtful of you to keep their drawings up. They will be so pleased when I tell them. They wanted to come with me today until they heard we were going to be watching golf on T.V."

"John, let's take the girls on a hike when the weather permits. They will love picking wildflowers. We can go to the butterfly sanctuary."

This sounds great to him. "You know just how to make my daughters happy. For having only known them a short time, you are resourceful and thoughtful in thinking of fun things for them to do."

The tournament is just starting. John is pleasantly surprised that Erika is enjoying the game. "Jennifer hated it when she had to endure watching golf for my sake. Have you ever played?"

"Oh yes, I've played the game, it's very challenging. You can take me out sometime."

John smiles, he can't believe he is so blessed to have a girlfriend who wants to play golf. "Now you're talking!"

She walks to the kitchen and brings in two tall drinks. A slice of lemon floats on top of each glass of iced tea. She is smart enough not to offer her Christian date a beer. She sits down next to him; he's unable to speak for a second. He takes a deep look into her entrancing eyes. "Erika, you are so beautiful, how did I get so lucky?"

Her comeback is, "You are not so bad yourself. I truly believe we make an outstandingly handsome couple."

John cautiously admits, "I have to be careful not to be prideful being next to you. I can't help but notice when we walk into a restaurant together that heads turn. I'm sure they are looking at you. That's just the way it is. Perhaps because we are both tall, people notice us. God can use us if we remain humble and not focused on our appearance."

Erika happily interrupts, "John, did you see that wedge shot? That was terrific how he got the ball out of the sand trap."

As they root for opposing players, Erika was hoping the competitor would win, but is pleased that John is happy.

A week later, it's a perfect day for golf and John has the afternoon off. Erika gets a call, "Are you ready to hit the links? I'll give you three strokes."

Erika's reply, "I'll take you up on that. What time should I be ready?"

"How about right after lunch? One o'clock?"

"Perfect, I haven't played for a while; it will be fun to get out."

When he pulls up to the cottage, he's surprised to see her ready and waiting. Her auburn hair is in a pony-tail under a white visor. Decked out in a white golf skirt and pale pink golf shirt, she looks gorgeous. She has the longest most beautiful legs he has ever seen. As John loads her white golf bag into the car trunk, he remarks, "What in the world is this, 'Taylor Made' clubs? Is this a joke? Are you a wanna-be, Erika?"

She tells him, "I want to look the part."

It's a perfect day, 74 degrees with low humidity. They arrive at the Catawba Golf Club. The views are breath-taking. Mowers have just finished, and the aromatic smell of fresh-cut grass fills the air. John pulls up in a white golf cart and Erika climbs in. Both sets of clubs are in the back. He has no clue about her golfing skills. She's held back on telling him she went to Tulane on a four-year golf scholarship. When the game is over, she has beaten him by four strokes. He loves her competitive spirit and loves being with her. Who knew a game of golf would seal the deal.

"You tricked me! A four-year golf scholarship, I walked into that. You certainly caught me by surprise. Erika, you have a great swing and your putting skills are amazing. You'll be a great golfing partner. It will keep me on my toes and sharpen up my game."

Weeks turn into months as John and Erika become closer. He sees her as loving, fun, kind and a good Christian. She has been helping at the church with the seniors. When Marty needs help in Kid Zone, she is always there to lend a hand. She makes John feel appreciated and respected. Several people who see John and Erika together have commented on what a handsome couple they are.

He tells her, "I'm so glad you're in my life." As time passes, they go on hikes and bike rides. They attend baseball games and church events. John and Erika have taken Taylor and Kim several times to McDonald's for lunch in the play gym area. Ice cream dates with his daughters every Sunday are routine. He can't help but notice how well Taylor and Kim relate to Erika. He feels very good about this. Erika is flawless in his eyes.

Often Mark and Heidi join them. They can see how in love John is. He deserves to be happy. Heidi's hoping for the best for John.

Both couples are getting serious. John feels Erika would be a wonderful mother for his daughters. He has fallen hard for her. Mark knows that Heidi is his soulmate. The two eligible bachelors have decided it's time for them to talk with their respective ladies about a deeper commitment.

At the law office, John and Mark are beginning to see a conclusion to a very challenging case. They are relieved when it ends in their favor. Now that it's over, they will take some time off to relax.

Surprise at the Lake

It is a perfect day to take the pontoon out on Lake Norman. Erika and Heidi get a call, "Would you two like to go out on the lake? How about packing a lunch to share on the boat?" Erika and Heidi come up with a menu suited for royalty: roast beef sandwiches with horseradish sauce, a tray of cheese and veggies, potato chips, large pitted Italian olives, and chewy brownies with walnuts. Mark has a cooler full of ice-cold Cokes. John is in charge of the music. He loves the old crooners and he will bring CDs of Eric Clapton singing "Wonderful Tonight," "Can't Help Falling in Love with You" by Elvis, and Frank Sinatra crooning "Fly Me to the Moon." John has brought other love songs. He's a romantic.

Erika and Heidi are on the porch waiting for them. It's a beautiful sunny day. The black Mercedes pulls up; the guys do a soft wolf call when they see them in shorts. Smiling in a joking way, they let the ladies know they look great. Heidi has on a red-and-white striped shirt with her khaki shorts. Erika's wearing a navy shirt with a white anchor silk screened on the front and white shorts. A large blue canvas bag is slung over her shoulder.

John asks, "What's in the bag, Erika?"

She tells him, "Camera, cell phone, sunscreen, sunglasses, and two beach towels. What were you expecting, a rattlesnake?"

John comes back, "Oh, you're real funny."

They all laugh; John hugs her.

As they approach the lake, they see a large sign decorated with sailboats, "Welcome to the Lake."

Mark says, "Hope that includes pontoons."

All of a sudden Erika remembers she forgot the sandwiches. They are still in the refrigerator. Before the Pontoon is loaded, they head back to 451 Palm Tree Lane to get the food. Erika is very embarrassed but allows John to tease her over the predicament. She's a good sport, John applauds her for it.

Retracing their path, soon they all get out on the lake. The water is calm. The two couples discuss the heavy traffic they can see on Interstate 77. Glad they are far from it, they drift even further west on the lake. John turns the music down now that the sound of traffic has faded. Erika and Heidi spread out the food; Mark serves the Cokes. Heidi compliments him on bringing diet colas for the ladies. They pose for pictures as romantic songs play. On occasion, waves from a jet ski rock the boat.

An older couple in another pontoon get a big kick out of the laughter from the two couples, as they enjoy their time together. They've been out on the lake for three hours. All the food's gone and several pictures have been taken. Now the big surprise.

John says, "Mark and I have a little gift for each of you." In a magical moment, each pulls out a sparkling diamond ring. Heidi is overcome with joy.

Erika says, "Are you serious?" She muses that her acting skills are that of a veteran actress. Heidi wasn't expecting the proposal, but Erika had been anticipating it every time she was with John. Both seem happier than words can express. Mark throws out the idea of a double wedding.

"What do you ladies think? John and I say, why not?"

The girls shrug. Heidi says, "Why not?" Erika doesn't care how or where they get married as long as it happens and she finally gets her prize. She figures that she's put in enough hard work. Erika schemes some private thoughts, "*A successful attorney ought to be able to afford a very large home for his wife.*" They get big hugs.

John says, "I'll call my parents. They will be happy to hear the news."

His mother takes the call. "That's wonderful. Certainly you and your friends can stop by tomorrow. We are anxious to meet our future daughter-in-law and Mark's fiancé. Is 2:00 okay? I'll make coffee and a special dessert."

He thanks his mom and says, "See you tomorrow."

Attorney Barringer suspects something when he overhears the conversation. "Diane, what's so exciting?"

She says, "Yes, John is getting married to this Erika he's been dating. He must really love her. It's time for him to settle down. He needs a wife and our granddaughters need a mom. Mark is also getting married and they are all coming over tomorrow for an introduction."

The next day, at exactly 2:00, John's Mercedes pulls through the gate at Whitney Chase. Shrubs are neatly trimmed around a cast-iron fountain. The sun shines on the water as it sprays into the air; a plump little robin flaps its wings on the edge of the fountain. Wide brick steps hold large pots of bright yellow marigolds. The Barringer's home is a flat front Georgian classic.

When the bell rings, Attorney and Mrs. Barringer welcome them. Mark has been like a son for years. John introduces Erika and Heidi. Diane Barringer tells them they'd like to be referred to as Diane and Edward. She invites them all to come into the family room where it's comfortable.

Erika is impressed with John's parents' fabulous home. Rich jewel tones accent the neutral furnishings. Heidi and Erika take a seat on the soft, light taupe leather sectional that faces the stone fireplace. A large black shiny Steinway grand piano fills up one corner of the room. It is covered with family photographs, some very old. John tells Erika how his mother is an accomplished classical pianist and once accompanied the New York philharmonic. Diane humbly responds, "Oh John, that was a long time ago. Now I just play for my own enjoyment."

John and Mark kick back on matching tweed wing-back chairs with footstools. Feeling at home, they kick off their loafers so they can put their feet up. Attorney and Mrs. Barringer relax in their favorite recliners.

All get acquainted with light conversation. Edward and Diane are interested in their jobs. Also, they want to be sure of each lady's faith. Diane is carefully listening and studying the gals. She has a sharp mind, as she is slow to speak and quick to notice. Erika sees John's mother as educated, sophisticated, and accomplished. Pretty and young looking for her age, she intimidates Erika. She's very different from her own mother. Erika hasn't seen her mother in years and has no desire to see her again.

Diane asks John to help her with dessert. In the kitchen, she quietly tells her son, "I want you happy John, but there's something about Erika that disturbs me. I don't think you should marry her." John reassures his mother that once she gets to know Erika that she will love her. Diane quickly realizes that her son has already made up his mind. The conversation ends.

Shortly, she brings in a tray of raspberry cheesecake. John carries in the coffee. After two hours, John makes the formal announcement. "We are planning a double wedding," Mark adds, "We've been bachelors long enough, especially me." Everyone laughs.

Edward is elated with the news. "Diane and I want to congratulate you fine couples. We want to see you all happily married."

"I am so pleased to have met you," Erika confirms.

John seems happy with his parent's response. Heidi compliments Diane on the cheesecake and thanks her. After another few minutes, Heidi and Erika help carry the plates to the kitchen. The young couples decide it's time to leave; they feel the visit went well.

Diane Has Doubts

After they leave, Diane tells Edward, "I see lots of good qualities in Heidi. Mark has found a solid Christian for a wife." Edward senses his wife is concerned about Erika. Diane has a worried look on her face as she tries to explain to her husband. She goes on to say, "There's something about Erika that bothers me. It's my women's intuition."

Edward sticks up for Erika. "Give her a chance, she's fine. Couldn't you see John is in love with her? We want our son to be happy, don't we? Our granddaughters need a mother. Diane, don't throw cold water on our son's plans. We will love and accept our new daughter-in-law as a daughter."

Diane doesn't want to be a spoiler. She wants to see her son happily married. So she draws back, not wanting to be negative, but that doesn't make her concerns go away. She has learned from the past, when you sense a 'red flag' going up, pay attention to it. Diane couldn't say that no woman would be ever good enough for their son, because they had both loved John's first wife, Amy, as their own daughter, even from the beginning. Something is very different about Erika. Perhaps Edward is right. They must give her a chance, Diane acquiesces.

When Heidi and Erika return home, Erika tells Heidi, "Mrs. Barringer loved you right away, I noticed that.

Heidi responds, "She liked you too. You just read her wrong. Erika, why are you so insecure?" Erika shrugs her shoulders.

Erika tells Heidi she was hoping John's mother might be the mother she never had. She begins to tell Heidi the story about her childhood. "It was painful. Mother made it clear she never wanted me; the abortion she planned failed. She controlled everything, if I didn't eat dinner it was served to me the next day or until I ate it. I would throw up. Under my bed was my safe place. There I would hide and cry. Mother had several men friends, and they abused me. When I'd tell her, she'd refuse to believe me. She would tell me to go live with my father if I wasn't happy there. Heidi, I never saw my father. Where was he? Who was he? Mother probably didn't know herself."

Heidi feels terrible for her. She can't comprehend a childhood like that. Perhaps that explains the reason for her rejection of God. Heidi asks, "How did your mother and her mother get along?"

Erika said, "They hated each other. Grandma was against tattoos, so my mother had both of her arms covered with ink."

Heidi can't understand why someone would hurt themselves to get even with someone else. Erika's eyes tear up as she brings up all the old pain. "Excuse me, Heidi, I'm going to my room." Quickly she changes into her pajamas, crawls into bed, and attempts to comfort herself. As Erika lies down to rest the phone rings. It's John.

"Hi honey, I was very proud of you today."

Erika inquires, "Did your parents approve of me?"

He is quick to answer, "My father loves you. You'll have to give my mom some time to get to know you."

"What are you saying, John? Your mom doesn't approve of me?"

"Erika, I love you. Mom doesn't really know you. I'm her only child so she's protective. There's nothing to be concerned about, trust me."

Erika has never mentioned her parents and has seemed to avoid the subject. John thinks it's time to bring them into the conversation. "When do I get to meet your parents?" Erika knew it would come up sooner or later. So she takes a deep breath and explains her horrific upbringing.

John is crushed to think this beautiful woman had to endure such atrocities. He lovingly assures her that all of that is behind her and that he will always protect her. Having this new knowledge of Erika's past makes John love her even more.

"We can talk tomorrow. Goodnight honey, I adore you."

Erika is slow to hang up the phone. Anger fills her thoughts; she can feel her blood pressure increasing. She rings her evil friend, "Nancy, do you want the good news first or the bad news?"

Nancy speaks up, "Give me the bad first."

"John's mother doesn't like me, just like Brian's mother. I will not let Diane Barringer get in the way of what I want and have worked so very hard for. I will show her that she's messing with the wrong person. She'll find out just how toxic I can be."

Nancy tells her, "We will give that old hag what she deserves. I have some great ideas. Small things, but they will add up. We'll make her look like she's losing her mind, forgetting everything. We'll cut off her head and watch her bleed. Start slow and let it build. Let's play games with her."

Erika remembers how Brian's mother prevented them from getting married. "The very thought of Brian's mother arouses my anger. I wonder how long it will eat away at me. Now John's mother is against me." Erika can't discuss this with John, she must conceal all her anger. Now his mother is on her hit list. She snickers as she contemplates getting even.

"Nancy, the good news is we are getting married. It's going to be a double wedding; Mark and Heidi will share the day. Can't talk long, it's getting late, but I wanted you to know." They hang up. Erika is furious! She's breathing heavily and can't relax and fall asleep. She now detests Diane Barringer. She'll get even with her.

John and Mark feel sure John's parents are happy with the news. The next morning, Heidi gets a call from Mark. "John and I would like you and Erika to include Diane in some of the plans. Your mothers both live out of state, so perhaps you could take Diane when you shop for wedding dresses? It would be nice to make her feel a part of things."

Erika explains to Heidi, "I really need to score some points with Diane. I'll call her." What she actually means is that destroying Diane is at the top of her agenda. The more she contemplates Diane's rejection of her, the more rage she feels.

Erika calls the Barringer house. "Hi Diane, Heidi and I would love to have you go with us to help select dresses for the wedding. Would you like to meet us at the bridal shop, the one in the Harris Shopping Center?"

Diane knows exactly where it is. "Thanks for inviting me, I would love to join you. I'll meet you both there. That will be Wednesday at one?" Erika confirms the day and time. Diane appreciates them including her. Erika purposely tells Diane the wrong day and she tells Heidi the correct day. This is the beginning of things to come.

Wednesday is here. Diane is dressed very casually in her new classic blue jeans and a beige linen blazer. She's comfortable in spike heels. As she drives to the bridal shop, she is so pleased her soon to be daughter-in-law wants her advice on which dress will look the best. Diane plans to be there at 1:00, she arrives a little early. After a pleasant conversation with the shop owner, she waits and waits. Soon it's one-thirty and they haven't shown up.

She tells the owner, "There must have been a mix-up in the plans. I'll double-check with my future daughter-in-law. I must have remembered the time wrong." She calls Erika's cellphone and it goes to voicemail. A message is left and she decides to leave. She's disappointed and concerned that she didn't remember the plan correctly. Erika has set in motion the first of many schemes that will cause Diane to doubt her own memory.

On Thursday Diane and her best friend Grace, an African American, meet at 'The Trade Winds' for lunch. Grace is Diane's prayer partner, her confidant, and she occasionally babysits the grandchildren. They have been close friends for over fourteen years. Grace prefers this restaurant because she can bring her dog. The two ladies are having lunch at a table on the sidewalk. Francey, Grace's beautiful white, standard poodle is lying under the table. At the next table, a well-behaved black lab is napping. The waiter has placed a bowl of water near the door for pets.

All of a sudden Diane gets a call from Erika, "Where were you today? Heidi and I waited an hour for you." There is sharpness in her voice.

Diane apologizes, "It was a mistake. I thought it was planned for Wednesday, I'm so sorry. I guess I got confused."

Erika's voice is abrupt and harsh, "We really wanted your opinion. Heidi and I chose the dresses ourselves."

Diane is concerned that she got the day wrong. She felt sure the day planned was Wednesday. She will let it slide, no reason to make a big deal out of it. Erika, on the other hand, feels good about getting the well-executed jab at her future mother-in-law. Getting even is so sweet to Erika, but she will always be subtle about it.

The next few weeks go by fast. Wedding plans are being arranged, today Erika will be close to finishing up. After two hours, she stretches out on her bed to relax. Exhausted, she dozes off into a deep sleep. A strange nightmare soon appears. A wedding is taking place in a large ornate cathedral in Paris. Many guests are seated to witness the marriage. Three faceless, tall slender bridesmaids wearing black gowns and carrying candle-lit white lanterns parade down the center aisle. As they arrive at the altar, they are paired up with three faceless, tall best men wearing black tuxedos with black bow ties. The organist is pounding the keys louder and louder, hurting Erika's ears. "HERE COMES THE BRIDE"! Just then Jennifer Davis appears. She is dressed in the purest white gown Erika has ever seen. It actually glows. Jennifer is carrying a white Bible as she floats down the aisle. Her feet aren't even touching the floor. She has the happiest smile on her face as she arrives at the altar. The groom turns to face his bride, it's John. The priest asks, "Does anyone object to this union?" Erika is terrified and abruptly screams, "I object! I object!" The quick reaction jolts her awake.

Feeling weak and washed out, the scary dream has sapped all of Erika's energy. With half-opened eyes she struggles to reach the bottle of sleep aids. She swallows two and flops down on her bed. Perspiration is dripping off her forehead as again she drifts off to sleep.

Two hours later she sits up in bed and shrugs off all the negative energy. Heidi is just getting home. Erika greets her with, "Good morning, glad you're home. We need to finalize a few details for our wedding. Are you nervous? I am, but we are so lucky to be marrying two successful attorneys."

Heidi speaks softly, "I don't think of it that way. We are marrying the men we love."

Erika tries to reword her remark, "Oh, you know what I mean. Of course, we love them, that's understood. Saturday will be here in no time. I see you picked up the baskets for our flower girls to carry down the aisle. Can you believe it's tomorrow?"

Double Wedding

Erika and Heidi have spent the past several weeks planning for the big day. Even though the wedding will be small, they have paid attention to details. Today is the big day, all arrangements have been made.

It is a perfect day for the wedding, sunny and 78 degrees. Down by the lake, a white arbor is trimmed with pink roses and dark-green English ivy. Diane, wearing a lovely soft pink linen suit, and Edward looking very handsome in his black tux, are seated. Family and friends are escorted to their seats. A popular disc jockey is playing 'At Last' by Etta James. Taylor and Kim are dressed in white organza dresses with wide pink satin ribbons as sashes around their waists. They walk down the aisle tossing pink rose petals out of white baskets.

Now an instrumental of the Bridal Chorus is playing. The two stunning brides are wearing taupe dresses, each tailored a little differently. Heidi's is an A-line tea-length dress with a sweetheart neckline and V-cut back. It is covered with sparkly Aztec designs. Erika's strapless solid organza dress has a trumpet silhouette with a gradually flared skirt and fitted bodice. She's dressed to accentuate her physical assets. Both brides look gorgeous!

Heidi and Erika walk thru the arbor, each carrying long-stemmed pink roses with sprays of white baby's breath. A gentle breeze comes off the lake. John and Mark, dressed in black tuxedos with taupe bow ties, stand proudly as they see their beautiful brides walk slowly towards them. Vows and soft kisses are exchanged. Their pastor announces, "Meet Mr. and Mrs. John Barringer and Mr. and Mrs. Mark Larson." 'Unforgettable' by Nat King Cole, plays. The two couples walk arm in arm toward the back. Soon they're exchanging hugs and receiving well-wishes from their guests.

Off to one side is a large round table covered with a long white linen cloth. In the middle of the table is a beautiful three-tiered wedding cake with two miniature bride and groom couples perched on top. On another tiered plate are dainty tea sandwiches and fancy mints. Delicate French Limoges white china plates are perfectly arranged on the table with embroidered ecru linen nap-kins. The two happy couples gather to cut and serve the cake. There are two other tables, both with long white cloths. One holds elegantly wrapped gifts. The other matching table holds an antique cut glass punch bowl. A slimmed-down Marty Scott looks classy in her soft pink dress as she serves the punch. She is carefully pouring the punch into each crystal cup. The guests enjoy finger sandwiches and strawberry champagne punch.

Edward has arranged for a portable dance floor. The two couples happily whirl and sway to the music, "The Way You Look Tonight". After they finish, their friends and family give a toast to the two beautiful couples. Most of the guests take turns on the dance floor. The last song, "For Once in My Life" by Stevie Wonder, plays. The whole group enjoys the last dance.

Attorney Edward makes an announcement. "We are happy for these two couples, may their love grow. Let the unions of Mark and Heidi, and John and Erika be blessed." Refreshments have been served and gifts opened.

John asks for everyone's attention; "We want to thank all of you for celebrating this special day with us. The four of us will be leaving early tomorrow for a brief honeymoon in California. We also want to thank Grace for volunteering to stay with Taylor and Kim while we are gone. The girls love staying with her."

The Honeymoon

Two rooms at the Four Seasons are on reserve for the new couples as they part ways for the evening. John carries his bride over the threshold. Happy that they are now alone, they share a toast with champagne. Before they fall asleep, John sets the alarm for early wakeup. They must catch the five-hour flight to San Francisco. He has reserved a car to drive the four of them south along the coast to Carmel.

John tenderly caresses Erika as they make love. He is so happy he's married to her. He pulls her close and falls asleep with her in his arms. Erika wishes she could fall asleep that easily. She lies there eyes wide open, being careful not to disturb her husband. The dream is back, is it a curse? Will this go away? Temporarily paralyzed by the image, it seems so real. She can never mention it to John. She'll try to force herself to ignore it but the ghost-like image of Jennifer clings to her memory. Jennifer looks so alive. Suddenly she remembers one medication that might help. Leaping out of bed, she rushes to her suitcase. Nervously she snaps off the cap and sixty-four little blue pills scatter on the floor. Desperately, on her hands and knees, she gathers them up. She swallows two and gulps down a large drink of water.

An hour later, the two tiny pills seem to help, she finally drifts off to sleep. Too soon the alarm goes off. John gently kisses his bride on the cheek. "Wake up Erika, we can't miss our flight. Mark and Heidi are meeting us at check-in."

"Oh John, I'm so tired." Slowly she drags herself out of bed, it's difficult just keeping her eyes open.

He urges her on, "Snap to it, Honey. You can sleep on the plane."

They arrive on time but the plane is late. John suggests coffee at an airport restaurant. "Mark, that family is leaving, let's grab their table." They politely weave their way through the crowd. John motions to the waitress, "We'll have four coffees. The ladies would like pecan rolls. We'll have glazed doughnuts, two each please, thank you." The waitress informs them, "Sugar and cream are on the table." The next hour goes fast; soon they will file out to the gate.

Erika's thoughts swirl, hoping once back home she can call Nancy. She will cast out the horrible image. She does not recognize the 'casting out' as spiritual. She doesn't question it. The only thing that matters is that the evil force goes away.

The two couples arrive at 'Carmel by the Sea'. The resort looks over the Pacific Ocean. It is breathtaking to see the waves crash against the rocky coast. Their rented suites have great views of the ocean. The rooms are furnished in white. Very contemporary abstract paintings enhance the walls. The artwork is neutral with large splashes of turquoise on each canvas—very stunning! The bathrooms look like a California spa. All of this will bring lasting memories.

Soon the two couples are dressed for the beach. Erika is in her sexy white bikini and Heidi is in her bright yellow bikini. They plan to spend a couple of hours each day lying on the beach. They run quickly on the hot sand to avoid burning their feet. On the large orange and white striped blanket, they toss down soft pillows to make it comfy. Heidi has brought a small radio to listen to classical music. The beautiful compositions are interrupted only by the crash of the waves and the sound of seagulls. Covered with suntan lotion, now and then they run to the water's edge to cool off.

Some of the time, John and Mark are riding the waves or playing volleyball on the beach with other hotel guests. Often they join their wives to relax. Mark playfully demands, "Move over girls, share the blanket."

After fun in the sun, they find time to hit the sophisticated shops. Erika spots a beautiful Gucci black shoulder bag for $2500 and a matching wallet for $450. She looks at John with a child-like pouting expression. He hesitates, but then nods that it's ok. Erika smiles as she thinks that this is going to work out just fine.

They have lunch on the beach and enjoy wonderful dinners at the hotel. Each evening the lovers find time for each other.

Erika comments, "We lose two days in the air, so this really is an eight-day honeymoon. Let's enjoy every minute, I love it here!"

When it's time to return to North Carolina, they each regret their time on the west coast has come to an end. They're sad to leave.

Wonderful memories follow them home. Upon return, Heidi and Mark will reside at Heidi's little cottage on Palm Tree Lane. John and Erika will be living in his home with Taylor and Kim. Grace is expecting them and the girls are expecting a surprise.

Grace meets John and Erika at the door. Taylor and Kim come running in from outside when they see their dad's car pull in. The girls greet them with hugs of joy. Kim says, "Did you bring us a surprise?"

"Absolutely! Erika, where did you pack the gifts for the girls?" Soon they are checking out their new baby blue hats with Carmel inscribed across the front in rhinestones.

Taylor says, "Thanks for the cute hats!" They run to see how they look in the mirror.

Grace asks, "How was 'Carmel by the Sea'?"

John responds, "Unbelievable! We had a spectacular time. I did miss my beautiful daughters, although I knew in my heart they were having a wonderful time with you."

Grace tells him, "Each evening before bed, I told the girls stories about a rabbit and a hedgehog. Taylor and Kim were spellbound with excitement. I had two hand puppets to make the stories come alive."

John says, "No wonder the girls love to have you stay with them. I really appreciate you, Grace."

Now with John and Erika home, Grace is ready for a break. She will be happy to go home to her own bed. John thanks her with a handsome check. Next, he phones his parents to let them know they are home. The call goes to voicemail. "Wanted you to know that we are back, had a great time, talk to you soon."

John's finding it difficult to acclimate back to a normal routine after enjoying the California resort. Now he shifts gears, it's morning and he's on the way to the store to get milk. Kim and Taylor are watching cartoons. Erika is on the phone with her evil friend. Nancy asks, "How was John's mother at the wedding?"

Erika says, "Thank God, she stayed out of my way. His father loves me."

Nancy questions, "How do you know that?"

Erika explains, "I enjoy joking with him, I compliment and flatter him, he loves it. Diane has ruined it with me. I do not forgive! I do not forget! I get even. That's how I'm wired. It won't be difficult because Diane is very naïve and trusting."

Nancy warns, "Settle down Erika. When you're getting even with her, always appear loving and kind, especially in front of John. Act like you're sticking up for his mother when in actuality you're sticking it to her. Who could question an innocent Christian that's so helpful at church?"

Erika hears the garage door, "Gotta run, Nancy."

John puts the milk in the refrigerator and grabs the newspaper.

The phone rings, Erika answers. It's Heidi, "Diane has invited us over this morning for brunch. Can John stay with the girls?"

Erika says, "Sure he can. I'd love to go. Can you pick me up?"

Heidi prefers the side entrance at the Barringer's home. Diane warmly greets them and escorts them into the kitchen. Erika notices Diane's house key on the hall table and quickly picks it up and puts it in her pocket.

Immediately they smell fresh banana nut bread just out of the oven. The round table in the breakfast room is beautifully set for three. A bowl of fresh fruit is on the counter; Erika tests a green grape.

Heidi notices Diane has her good china and silver out, "What pattern are these?"

Diane replies, "It's Golden Florentine by Wedgewood. It's English. The silver is Francis I by Reed and Barton. They were both my grandmother's and I treasure them. I'm glad you appreciate it."

Heidi tells her, "They are elegant." Heidi respects Diane and genuinely likes her; she has no idea Erika is planning her harm.

Erika excuses herself to grab a sweater from the car so she can put the key in the door lock. Cleverly, accomplishing her task, she rejoins them with an innocent smile on her face.

"I want you both to know how pleased I was with the wedding ceremony," says Diane. "It was simple, small, and elegant. Erika, I'm so happy, you complete our family. Taylor and Kim now have a mom. I'm thankful. Welcome to our family. I'll love you as my own daughter." It takes every ounce of strength for Erika to restrain the anger that is seething inside of her. She forces out a "Thank you."

Diane smiles, "Tell me about Carmel by the Sea, that California paradise." Both ladies excitedly tell Diane all about the decorum, food, and the ocean. Diane replies, "I'm so glad you enjoyed it."

Heidi compliments Diane on how good the banana nut bread is. Diane asks, "Can I pour you a second cup of coffee?"

Just then, Erika reaches over to get the sugar. As she stretches out her arm, she knocks over the cream pitcher. Cream runs off the edge of the table and all over Diane's navy-blue skirt. Erika acts like it was an accident and apologizes, "Oh, I'm so sorry."

Diane is gracious, "No big deal, I'll go change."

While she is gone, Heidi tells Erika, "Diane's birthday is this Wednesday; the fellas are planning a surprise get-together. Shhhhh, here she comes." The conversation turns toward the granddaughters. They talk about Taylor and Kim and how well they're doing in school. Diane shares some cute stories.

Erika checks her watch, it's almost time for her nail appointment. Before leaving they thank Diane for the delicious brunch. Heidi thought it was a pleasant visit, but Erika is elated that's it's over.

As the women step onto the side portico to leave, Diane notices her house key is in the door lock. She is embarrassed and wonders how she could have left it there. She believes it must have been there all night. Edward would start to worry about her if he knew.

Diane enjoyed being with Erika and Heidi. She has been able to push her negative thoughts aside and accept Erika.

John knows his mother didn't accept his wife before they were married; he decides that all he can do is hope that their relationship will improve. Knowing what a strong Christian his mother is, he feels sure she will eventually accept Erika and see what a wonderful person she really is.

It's not that simple for Erika, pretending to be a Christian, but she knows that she can pull it off as long as she doesn't have to be around his mother. John's in love and oblivious to Erika's anger and bitterness. She thrives on it and Nancy is eager to coach her onward.

When Erika returns home, John has questions for his wife. "Did my mother make you feel comfortable?" Erika makes John believe she was treated badly. "Your mother directed all the conversation to Heidi. It was like I wasn't even there. It was very hurtful."

John is surprised to hear that. "Really? That is not like my mother. Do you want me to have a talk with her?"

Erika tells him, "Wait and give me a chance to win her over. Talking to her will only jeopardize my chance at a relationship with her." John agrees to wait. He has confidence in his wife.

Diane's Birthday

He continues to plan his mother's surprise birthday party. The guys want to make it special. Mark has a great idea, "John, your mom was born and raised in Houston right?"

John says, "Yes, and she graduated from the University of Texas."

Mark tells him the idea, "I found an older C.D. I've had, 'The Yellow Rose of Texas'. I thought we could play it at the party."

John adds, "You won't believe this. She loved that song when she was young. No kidding, it was her favorite! Can you believe her favorite flower is still the yellow rose?"

Mark is pleased to hear that. "Heidi and I will give her two dozen yellow roses. This will be perfect." They get all of their plans organized for the special evening and invite a few of her friends.

On the day of her birthday, everyone gets there early before Diane gets off work. Diane isn't expecting cars in the drive when she gets home. She walks in after a long day of volunteering at the hospital. "Surprise! Happy Birthday, Diane!" shouts the whole group. Grace is happy for her best friend and prayer partner. Just then,

John turns on the 'Yellow Rose of Texas' CD. Everyone stands, singing, and clapping to the rhythm of the song. Some are dancing. Everyone is smiling and having a great time. Diane is thrilled as she joins in on the fun as they sing the entire song.

Next, John speaks up; "Taylor and Kim want to sing Happy Birthday to their grandmother. The tempo is a big contrast as their soft, sweet voices sing in front of their grandmother. A precious scene, Diane has a loving smile on her face as she hugs her granddaughters. "You have touched my heart."

The girls have been permitted to hand out the gifts to Diane. Taylor and Kim slip into the front bedroom where the presents are hidden. As Diane looks up, she sees Taylor very carefully carrying in a full vase of beautiful yellow roses. She tells her grandmother, "This is a gift from Mark and Heidi."

Diane says, "How beautiful, thank you. My favorite flower is the yellow rose. Taylor, please set them on the coffee table. You did a good job carrying that big vase, Honey."

Now it's Kim's turn to hand her grandmother a gift. "This is from Grace, Grandma!" Diane unwraps the neatly wrapped pink present to find a book by Erwin Lutzer. She is thrilled, "Thank you Grace, I've been wanting this book."

Taylor then hands her grandmother a shiny red gift bag from Erika and John. Diane pulls out the tissue paper, out slips a silver chain with a large medallion. Heidi is stunned since it is a necklace that Erika wore to the brunch. Erika had even commented that it was cheap and that she never liked it. Diane knows that John is unaware that the necklace had once belonged to his wife. Being kind, she thanks them for the gift.

Lastly, Kim hands her a small black box with a silver velvet bow. She says, "It's from Grandpa!" Diane is surprised to see a gold tennis bracelet with sparkling diamonds. She hugs her husband, "Edward this is wonderful, thank you." There are special birthday cards from others.

On the breakfast room table everything is set up for dessert. Colorful "Happy Birthday" paper napkins are neatly folded beside the glass plates. Lemon cake and French vanilla ice cream will be served. Mark proclaims, "This has to be my favorite cake."

Diane has given her sweet granddaughters permission to blow out the candles. Taylor and Kim, on the count of three, blow as hard as they can. The candles are blown out.

Taylor waves her little hands in the air to make the smoke go away. "Grandma, that's a lot of candles."

Diane tells her, "You did such a good job." Edward shares some funny family stories. It is a lot of fun, a great way to end the evening. Diane gets their attention, "You made my birthday special; I want to thank you all." Taylor and Kim are getting sleepy. Kim is rubbing her eyes and Taylor is yawning. John is hoping to leave soon.

Heidi takes charge of clean up and puts the dishes in the dishwasher. Erika gets busy putting the ice cream away. Turning her wedding ring around, a trick she learned years ago, she opens the freezer and makes a gouge on the stainless handle with her diamond.

Soon everyone is gone. Diane notices the mark on the freezer door handle. "Edward, look at this, there's a gouge on the handle. Erika was the one that got the ice cream out and put it away."

Edward comes to Erika's defense, "Oh no! Don't blame her! She would never do that on purpose."

Diane knows he favors Erika, she can do no wrong. He would never believe her. He pulls his wife over to him and gives her a soft kiss, "I love you, birthday girl. Don't fret. We will get it buffed out."

She lets her husband know it was a terrific birthday, "Thanks Honey, it was a wonderful party."

Diane decides she will not let it become a problem. She prays, "Dear Lord, remove my negative thoughts. Help me to see the best in Erika."

On the drive home, John comments to Erika, "I enjoyed the evening. My mother certainly appreciated all we did. She loved reminiscing to that ole Texas song."

With acute brevity, she responds, "It was nice. Look, John, the girls have fallen asleep in the back seat. It's too early for them to go to bed. Let's have a family night when we get home. Taylor and Kim have been working on special pictures in their coloring books. The girls will probably want to finish them before they go to bed." Erika knows how to score points with John—be good to his little girls.

Cramer Calls

Later that evening a call comes in from the hospital, it's Cramer. "Erika, we need you to work tomorrow." John can see her frustration building, her nostrils spread as her breathing becomes heavier. For a few seconds, there's silence.

She asks, "What shift are you referring to?"

Cramer says, "The early shift, we have four nurses that have called off sick."

Erika hesitates, but soon gives in, "I'll be there at seven in the morning."

"Can we depend on you?"

She snaps back, "I told you, I'll be there."

John is surprised by her sharp answer. He goes back to reading the Wall Street Journal. His daughters color on the floor near his feet. Now and then they interrupt to ask his advice on color selection. Kim asks, "Is blue a good color for the bow, Daddy?"

"Perfect," John reassures her. "Girls, let's get your night snack, it's almost your bedtime. Please put your coloring books away."

Erika announces, "Be sure they brush their teeth and say their prayers."

John answers, "We will get it all done."

Erika wants to pretend how much she cares for his daughters' welfare. He believes she's sincere. "I'm impressed with how well you care for the girls, Erika."

Still unhappy that she must go to work tomorrow, Erika stomps upstairs. Changing into her shiny white satin pajamas, she's ready for bed. She hollers down to John, "Honey, I'm going to bed, I have to get up at 5:30, "good night, John."

He calls back, "Good night Erika, I love you."

She removes the cap on the sleep aid bottle. Swallowing two pills, she gulps down water. She places the glass of water and pills back on the nightstand. Climbing into bed and pulling the fluffy yellow blanket up around her shoulders, she snuggles in. After a few deep breaths, she relaxes into a lazy stupor. The vision of Jennifer flashes in her mind momentarily, then the sleep aides kick in. She is sound asleep, never noticing when John comes to bed. Seven hours later the alarm blasts off, John doesn't hear a thing. Erika is furious. Still drowsy, she reaches over to slam on the snooze button. In doing so, she knocks over the glass of water on the nightstand, "Damn it." Exasperated, she gets out of bed. Now she's genuinely irritated as her feet land on wet soggy carpet, "Oh shit." John doesn't stir. He had hoped his wife would become a stay-at-home mom, but Erika needs her freedom.

The day is off to a bad start. Unwilling to change her attitude, she feels better when taking her frustrations out on inanimate objects. She slams down the mouth wash bottle, slams her hair brush down and the can of hair spray. Now dressed for work, she turns to go downstairs. Her sweater gets caught on the bedroom doorknob. Extremely annoyed, she frees herself. In the kitchen, she gets her to-go thermos and fills it with coffee. Grabbing a pastry, she heads out to work. Her patience is short. While driving, two cars blow their horns as she rudely cuts them off. Trying to replace her coffee in the holder half of it spills. Fortunately, it missed her scrubs. Parking in Jennifer's former spot gives her pleasure.

Entering the hospital she passes two colleagues in the hall, but she's not in the mood to acknowledge them. When the elevator opens, she ignores a doctor who is exiting. Finally calming down, she meets Cramer at the desk in I.C.U. "Thanks for coming in Erika. Our beds are full, you'll be busy."

"Yes Sir." She gets busy and cooperates.

When the shift ends, Cramer thanks her again. "You were a big help, Erika."

Before she can leave, Cramer confronts her about participating in the annual hospital calendar fundraiser.

"The hospital sponsors a calendar with pictures of hospital staff. The proceeds go to the children's cancer wing. Would you consider taking on this project?" Cramer asks hopefully. "I can give you all the details, I'll text you."

"Sure Cramer, I'm happy to help". She hurries out the door, anxious to go home after a long shift.

On the way home she texts John to check in. He quickly responds, "The girls and I have dinner all ready and we are going to do clean up so you can rest."

Erika speaks up, "Wow, you guys are great! I'll be home soon." Anxious to get there, she's driving thirteen miles over the limit. Suddenly she sees blue lights flashing, "Oh no, this time he has me." She pulls over to the curb, a scene all too familiar to her.

A tall slender patrolman walks up to her Nissan. "Do you know how fast you were going?" He notices her scrubs. Before she can reply he asks, "Do you work at the hospital?"

Erika sheepishly responds; "Yes Sir, I'm an ICU nurse." That tactic has never failed her.

He comes back with a warning, "I'm going to let you go, now slow down Ma'am." She thanks him and continues home.

After dinner she thanks John and the girls as she relaxes on the sofa. Sitting down next to her, he puts his arm around her. "I'm crazy about you Erika, and I'm sorry today was difficult."

"Thanks Honey, coming home to you is the best part of the day. I'm glad you weren't disturbed this morning. Good thing you're a sound sleeper." Erika doesn't tell him about getting pulled over for speeding. After all, she is his perfect wife.

Remembering her agreement to help Cramer with the calendar, Erika decides to start planning. Struggling to come up with a unique theme, she decides to call Nancy for ideas. Nancy has the perfect plan, take advantage of the Barringer's fabulous home for the calendar photos and maybe in the process find time to irk Diane.

The next day it's raining and the sky is dark and ominous. Not letting the weather deter her, she dials up her mother-in-law. Diane has no problem allowing Erika to take the calendar photos in her home. "I'm happy to help you out Erika." Erika grabs her red rain jacket and flips the hood over her head. Arriving at Diane's, she removes her wet boots before entering. Her mother-in-law offers some great ideas. Erika is impressed; she wants Cramer to be thrilled with the results.

Diane has a chocolate cake on the counter, and she offers her a slice. "Would you like vanilla ice cream on your cake?" She pours two cups of tea. On a pink plate, there are lemon wedges. They enjoy the dessert and visit awhile.

Erika checks her watch, then leaves to pick up Taylor and Kim. "Thanks, Diane, for your ideas. Is it okay with you if we take the photos tomorrow?"

She replies, "No problem, I'm happy to help."

The following morning a truck and a van arrive, carrying photo equipment, props, and staff. Twelve nurses, a few physicians, and 20 staff members are to be photographed. The photographer hauls in his equipment and the truck is unloaded. The crew stream in the front door and Diane is in shock. It looks like a large production on a Hollywood set. Erika never mentioned any of this.

The nurses want to primp so Diane leads them to her dressing room. Her allergies flair up as powder, hairspray, and perfume fill the air. Gasping for air, she runs out so she can breathe.

They gather in Edward's library. Some of the furniture in the library is relocated. Erika clears the important papers off of Edward's desk and recklessly shoves them in a drawer. His black leather love seat is moved over beside the stately tall grandfather clock. The carved walnut partner's desk is slid sideways three feet. A fire is started in the grand limestone fireplace. The two textured, beige, barrel-back side chairs are put in place on the Oriental rug.

The scene is set, the nurses are instructed on where to stand or sit. The photographer is very careful as he moves his equipment on the polished oak floors. Erika shoves his heavy black box, scratching the floor. She is careless and unapologetic.

Diane is surprised by the number of people and her furniture being rearranged. Erika had told her that there would only be a few nurses and simple photography set-up. She decides to say nothing about it, despite the inconvenience.

Suddenly the front doorbell rings, Erika welcomes Cramer in. He is impressed with the Barringer's home and listens to her clever ideas.

More pictures are taken. "I was so curious when I heard about the shoot, I couldn't stay away. I'm very pleased. Carry on, good job, Erika." She walks to the door with him as he leaves.

Edward is happy to have missed the whole scene. He left early for his day at Rotary. After an intense morning, all photos are taken. Diane successfully hides her disappointment in Erika and helps the photographers.

The guests are appreciative and comment on how lucky Erika is to have such a wonderful mother-in-law. Filming finishes and the crew moves all the furniture back in place. The equipment is removed and put back in the truck.

Erika wants everyone's attention, "Please be sure you haven't left anything in the dressing room. Oh, and I want to take you all to lunch as a thank you." She turns to her mother-in-law, "Thanks for allowing us to use your home, we are all leaving for lunch. When you get a chance, go to Main Street Café for a club sandwich, they are delicious."

Realizing she is not going to be included for lunch, Diane is hurt and embarrassed. A crew member notices and quietly asks her to go with them, but Diane feels that she is not wanted. She politely declines; besides, she needs to stay and repair the scratch Erika made on the office floor. Next, she takes on the impossible task of trying to reorganize her husband's papers on his desk. She knows Edward will be understanding and fix the mess.

Diane is taken aback by her daughter-in-law's insensitivity. She's hoping Erika did not do it intentionally and would like to give her the benefit of the doubt. However, she is wondering how long she can capitulate. It won't do any good to tell Edward. He'd give Erika a pass anyway. Diane puts the ordeal behind her. There is nothing important enough to store up negative thoughts. She tries to keep her mind uncluttered.

Harvard Seminar

At the law office the next day, Edward receives an announcement in the mail, a seminar at Harvard Law School is coming up. He will take it home to discuss with Diane.

"Oh Edward, this will be great! Should I make reservations for three couples? It would be good for John and Mark both to attend. What do you think, Honey?"

He depends on his wife's input; Edward has great respect for her. He agrees, "Let's all go. Heidi and Erika will enjoy the weekend."

Diane says, "They can go shopping with me. I'll call Grace, I hope she will be available to stay with Taylor and Kim."

Grace is always eager to spend time with John's daughters. They keep her young. There's a new playground with a big curvy slide, climbing bars and some of the swings have safety bars for young children. She will take Taylor and Kim there after school.

Meanwhile, Edward tells Diane, "John and Mark can tell their wives about the trip to Cambridge. Shall we stay at the Crandall Hotel?"

Diane says, "Oh yes, I love that hotel. It's quaint and romantic. The rooms are cozy, like you're in a home, not a hotel. We have always stayed at the Crandall when we are visiting Harvard."

Heidi and Erika are excited, they pack three days early. Erika opens her grey luggage on the bed. She selects a couple of sexy outfits she'll need for the weekend. Her new white cashmere sweater will be perfect for evenings. She feels sure there will be a pool at the hotel; the new black designer bikini she bought in Carmel goes in next. Her beautiful fuchsia dress will be perfect for dinner; she almost forgot her new gold Gucci belt.

Heidi packs her bag, casual navy slacks with a turquoise sweater for evening. A crisp white blouse will look good with her glen plaid pants. Her silk suit will be appropriate to wear to dinner. She'll need her yellow bikini.

Erika asks John, "Is your suitcase packed?" He reminds her, "Don't worry about me, I traveled a lot for business, it seems like I'm always packed."

Diane has finished packing for her and her husband. A few days later they arrive at the airport.

After a pleasant late afternoon flight, they're all gathered at the Hertz Rental Car counter to rent a Cadillac Escalade. They load the luggage and file in. Edward asks, "Diane, where is my leather briefcase? You said you had it." Diane, with a stunned look says, "I know that I put it in the overhead bin right above our seat." Little did she realize that Erika had moved it to another overhead bin five seats down the aisle.

John reassures his dad that they can call the airlines once they reach their hotel. "They will deliver it to your room, problem solved." Edward is relieved but is concerned his wife didn't remember which bin she put it in.

Edward says, "It isn't that late, I would like to take all of you to a little diner. You have to treat yourself to the best cherry pie on the East Coast, it's tart and packed with cherries." When they enter the diner, a middle-aged waitress leads them to a circular booth. Edward notices her name on her badge.

"Marie, how are you this evening?" She smiles and welcomes them. In total agreement, he orders six slices of cherry pie with ice cream. Then he adds, "Marie, is it possible to warm the pie?"

The answer comes back, "No problem."

After they finish, they agree the pie was fabulous!

For tomorrow, Diane wonders if the girls would like to go to antique shops and art galleries. Erika decides clothing stores would appeal to her. Heidi likes the idea of an art gallery and the antique shop intrigues her. "I love unusual art décor" she says.

Diane is anxious to show them around. "Tomorrow we'll visit all the unique shops. I'm sure you will find something you like. There is a lot to see."

Now the group heads for the Crandall Hotel where they have a late arrival. Everyone is ready for a good night's sleep.

The next morning they're up early. It's a beautiful sunny day. After breakfast they get ready for the day. The men have gone to the Harvard campus to listen to a lecture on "Advanced Bankruptcy." Diane shows her daughter-in-law and Heidi where all the best shops are.

Going from store to store, they peruse the interesting merchandise. Diane and Heidi are slightly disappointed as Erika takes up most of the time trying on clothes. They waited for what seemed like hours as she pranced in front of dressing room mirrors. Patience was wearing thin, but no one mentions it.

The shops and sidewalk cafés are filled with college students. Some are having quick snacks; others seem to be enjoying coffee as they check their notes for class. As with any college town, there is a lot of hustle and bustle. It's a youthful, fun atmosphere. Their last stop is a shoe store. No surprise, Diane and Heidi return to the hotel with new shoes. Erika returns with three outfits and four pairs of shoes. Diane had a pleasant day with her daughter-in-law and feels she is making headway with her.

The plan is for all to meet at seven for dinner. Edward has made reservations at a five star French restaurant. He knows the women will appreciate the ambiance.

Diane is ready on time, wearing periwinkle blue chiffon, tea-length dress. The color of her dress brings out the blue in her eyes. She has her tennis bracelet on and a small gold cross hangs around her neck on a delicate chain. She looks beautiful.

Heidi is smashing in a soft yellow silk suit with seed pearls sewn on the collar. She dresses conservatively with small pearl earrings.

Erika is radiant in her fuchsia dress; her wide gold belt shows off her twenty-four-inch waist. Her hair is in a French twist, allowing her brilliant rhinestone drop earrings to stand out. She is proud of her reflection in the mirror. The expense to get her hair done by the top stylist at the hotel was worth every penny. She is determined to upstage Diane. The women look stunning. Edward says, "You three are the best-looking ladies in the place."

Edward has requested the table by the window. It has a great view of the pond. Under the lavender flowers and lily pads, orange koi fish dart to and fro. The hostess tells them "We've given you the best table." The lovely tablescape is covered with a pristine white linen cloth with matching linen napkins. In the center of the table are two white candles and fresh multicolored flowers. Soon, a handsome server walks up to their table.

"Welcome, my name is Luke. I'll be your server." John helps his wife read the French menu. After their orders are complete, the waiter brings six tall glasses of ice water with lemon. Edward is about to say grace. He asks, "Luke, is there anything you would like us to pray for?"

"Thank you for asking. My father was diagnosed with lung cancer this week." Edward says, "I'm sorry to hear that." He asks his son to pray. John begins, "Heavenly Father, we worship you. Thanks for all you have entrusted to us. Be with Luke's father as he goes through this difficult time. We pray for healing. Bless this meal in Jesus's name, Amen."

Luke thanks them. After a delicious dinner, the three couples go out to the garden. They want a closer look at the lily pond and the large orange fish before turning in.

John wants them all to know, "This has been a fabulous evening."

After a good night's rest, they are all up and ready to go. It's another sunny day. John suggests, "Let's go enjoy a continental breakfast in the hotel."

Mark takes this opportunity to thank the Barringers for including Heidi and him. It's been a great experience.

Edward says, "Any pancakes left guys?" They all enjoy a wonderful breakfast.

Heidi comments on how nice Diane looks. "I remember when you bought that leopard print dress, it's stunning on you. Leopard never goes out of style, it's here to stay I do believe."

Edward is checking the time. The three attorneys have another seminar this morning. Keeping up to date on new laws is very important. Edward reminds them, "We have twenty minutes before the lecture begins, so we'd better get over to campus. We'll see you gals later." The women all walk out together.

Diane decides not to go shopping today. She'll go to the gym in their hotel. After that, a long hot shower will feel great.

Erika and Heidi are anxious to shop again. Erika is hoping the luxury purse she saw yesterday is still there. "Let's go to the Louis Vuitton store where I saw that purse. I should have grabbed it yesterday."

As the morning moves on, the gals head back to the hotel. Erika is pleased with her purchase. "I'm thankful the purse was still there. I won't let John know how much it cost, it was worth the $2,200. He's probably forgotten about the expensive Gucci bag he bought me in Carmel."

Heidi is more practical; a purse with that price tag wouldn't be an option. She finds Erika's spending spree ridiculous. She thinks of a saying that fits her perfectly: "People buy things they don't need, with money they don't have, to impress people they don't like."

She wouldn't repeat this to Erika because it would come off as hurtful and judgmental, but that doesn't stop her from thinking it. Heidi feels some things are best unspoken. Heidi feels we must look at God's word. II Corinthians 4:18 clearly states: For the things which are seen are temporal; but the things that are not seen are eternal.

Back at the hotel, they enter the newly remodeled lobby. Heidi comments on the décor, "You can easily tell this was put together by a professional. It has an old-world feel with a touch of modern." The aroma of freshly brewed coffee entices them to have a cup. Comfortable lounge chairs are the perfect place to sit and enjoy their cups of coffee. Heidi is observing the room. She took one semester of interior design, so it all makes sense to her. She appreciates good taste.

"Erika, do you like the hexagon pattern of the fabric on the furniture?

Erika comments, "Only you would notice that."

Heidi adds, "The three shades of green go well with the original dark walnut paneling. It's very art deco!"

Huge potted palms stand tall in large ivory-colored pots. An enormous reproduction of the well-known painting, *The Broken Pot,* hangs over the sofa in a heavy gold frame. On the tables are large squatty lamps with ivory colored shades. The bases are globe-shaped ivory porcelain, which replicates the shape of the potted palms. Antique art deco wall sconces and ceiling fixtures are original to the hotel, which was built in the 1920s. Large arched windows allow the sun to stream in. Heidi enjoys taking it all in as she relaxes. Erika has finished her coffee and Heidi goes for a refill. Gathering up her purchase, Erika heads for the stairs. Suddenly a loud voice bellows over the intercom, "Evacuate! Evacuate! Fire! Fire!"

Hotel Fire!

The announcement is terrifying. A fire! Their hearts pound with fear, they are in shock.

Heidi hollers to Erika, "Go warn Diane! I'll call Mark. Please hurry!"

Erika is halfway up the stairs. She wants to grab her cell phone that she left in the room by mistake. She hears the shower running as she passes Diane's room. She rushes back down to safety without warning her mother-in-law.

Heidi loves Diane and is very concerned. She sees Erika back in the lobby. "Did you tell Diane?" Erika tells her, "She will be here any moment." The three attorneys are returning from their seminar just as sirens begin to blow. Loud fire trucks are zooming up the street with red lights flashing. Guests and locals have gathered on the sidewalk. The three attorneys are in disbelief when they get to the scene.

Heidi is the first one they see, she is in a panic. "John, I can't find your mom. Erika went up to warn her but I haven't seen her yet." Edward has a frightened look on his face. He screams out to the firemen, "Please hurry! My wife is in room 206 on the second floor."

They rush over to the emergency crew for help. Heidi's eyes fill with tears. Her hands are damp with perspiration when she realizes flames can be seen on the second floor. Without concern for themselves, three firemen rush to find the missing woman.

Smoke is pouring into the hallway. They hear water running in the bathroom. Soon they find Diane on the floor of the shower overcome with smoke. They pull her out and wrap her in a towel. The medics rush her to their truck where vital signs are checked. The stretcher is hoisted into the ambulance.

Edward is a nervous wreck. John tries to comfort him. Engines are revving up and red flashing lights swirl as the siren blows. The whole scene makes it even more frightening. Heidi and the family climb into their large rented Escalade. Mark is at the wheel as they speed to the hospital. Not a word is spoken, Edward quietly prays.

An overwhelming sense of fear fills the vehicle as they travel. The tension can be cut with a knife. Mark pulls up to the door so the family and Heidi can exit before he parks. Diane is still in the emergency room. They gather in the waiting lounge. Forming a circle, they hold hands to pray. Hours later, the doctor tells them, "We almost lost her, I saw you all praying. There's power in prayer. She will be staying a few days for observation. We are moving her to ICU for closer monitoring. ICU is on the third floor."

Heidi pushes the button for the elevator. The door opens and Erika jumps in while the others stand back. A young girl in a wheelchair and her mother have to maneuver their way around Erika to get off the elevator. John squinches his eyebrows and shakes his head in disgust. Erika sarcastically responds in a snarky voice, "Well, paaardon me!" They arrive at the third floor and walk down the large polished hall to the double doors of the ICU. Erika almost slips as she walks on the shiny floor. John rings the buzzer to gain access to the unit.

In her room, they gather to pray again, this time to give thanks that Diane's life was spared. Immediately they realize Erika is missing.

Meanwhile, she is in a bathroom down the hall talking to Nancy, "No, I didn't warn her of the fire. I don't want her in my life. They think their prayers were answered, but mine weren't. I better go Nancy, I'll call you later."

The next day the doctor announces, "Mrs. Barringer can go home today. We see no signs of complications." The family is relieved. Edward makes a statement, "Start packing, we are all going home. To God be the glory, Diane is okay." With a sigh of relief he says, "North Carolina will look marvelous, better than ever before."

Going Home

Erika is disappointed that this opportunity was missed. She tells her husband, "I'm happy your mother is going to be okay." She has mastered lying while smiling. He acknowledges her comment with a squeeze of her hand and a caring smile. It pleases John; he sincerely believes Erika wants his mother to be okay.

The following day is Wednesday which means Diane is home in time for the ladies' prayer meeting. She is grateful and gives thanks to God for His faithfulness. Before she leaves for the meeting, she changes into her navy slacks and navy and white striped shirt. Her red leather belt is buckled around her trim waist. Soon she enters the church and goes to the conference room.

The usual faithful group of ladies are seated. Diane is glad to be back at Lakeside, she thanks the group for praying for her. "I'm grateful that God cares for us and protects us. I was told it was a close call, praise God, I've recovered. He is good. Now let's wrap up loose ends of our recipe book. All proceeds will go to support our missionaries. Thanks to all of you for your participation."

The ladies gather around the long table sorting through the stacks and organizing pages according to theme. There are photos for some of the recipes, which will make the book more appealing. All typed pages are laid out and taped down. Grace speaks up, "This project is coming together nicely. Do you all approve of the cover I designed?" Everyone is happy, everyone except Bessie.

With a disgusted look on her face, Bessie Hatfield speaks up. "I tested random recipes for the book and there was one that turned out terrible. Diane your name was on it, you must have left out some ingredients."

Diane is gracious, "Sorry Bessie, there must have been a mix-up. We'll check the ingredients and fix any mistakes. Thanks for bringing it to our attention, we want the book to meet the expectations of those who purchase it."

Grace privately tells Diane that she knew it wasn't her mistake. "Erika gave me the recipe with your name on it. She may have retyped it and left out a few ingredients. Do you think she would do that?"

Diane reminds Grace, "Erika is married to my son. I can't make a big deal out of it. If she did change it to make me look bad I have to overlook it." Grace understands, she nods her head. The recipe book is corrected, finalized, and ready for print. Marty Scott volunteers to drop it off at the printers.

Diane takes a deep breath and relaxes; happy the book is finished. She joins the others for prayer. Later they leave to go home for the night.

Erika Targets Taylor

It's a new day, John's at the office. Erika and Kim are in the kitchen ready to leave for school. Taylor isn't feeling well. She tells her stepmother, "I have the chills and a sore throat. It hurts to swallow Mommy; can I stay home today?" Erika, in a demanding voice, says, "I believe you're faking, get dressed. You're going to school; get your blue jeans and a white tee-shirt on. You are looking for an excuse." Erika is still reeling that her mother-in-law made it through the fire.

Taylor turns to go back upstairs, she's moving slowly. Her stepmother reinforces the demand, "Get a move on it, girl! You're going to make Kim late for school too if we have to wait for you. I do not want any excuses. You know how to test my patience!"

Just then John happens to call. "Erika, I'm glad I caught you before you left. Will you please drop off my briefcase on your way home? How's Taylor? Last night, she said it hurt to swallow. Did you check her temperature?" Erika says, "She's fine, she wants to go to school. She must be feeling better. You caught me just in time; we were getting ready to leave. I'll drop off your briefcase."

Two hours later, the school calls Erika, no answer. John gets a call from the school nurse. "Mr. Barringer, please come over to the school. Taylor needs to see a doctor." John tried in vain to get a hold of his wife. Canceling an important appointment, he calls the doctor in hopes they can fit Taylor in.

When John arrives at school; the nurse has Taylor ready to be excused in her father's care. "Her fever is 102, I am very concerned. Thanks for getting her so soon." John lets her know, "I appreciate your concern, thank you." His daughter is unusually quiet as they drive to the doctor. "Is your throat still sore?"

"Yes Daddy, it hurts to swallow." On the drive to the doctor's office, they pass by the Grand Roman Spa and John notices Erika's car in the parking lot.

Twenty minutes later, he walks into the Hoffman Medical Center with his daughter. Taylor is given a throat culture for strep. The doctor discusses it with John. "Good thing you brought her in, she has a severe case. If not attended to it could harm her heart or kidneys. I've had patients that thirty years later have had kidney transplants. Here are the instructions. I want Taylor on an antibiotic." The doctor tells Taylor, "I want you to rest when you get home."

"Yes sir."

Shortly father and daughter enter the parking area. John says to Taylor, "How about ice cream before we go home?"

Taylor feels sure ice cream won't be hard to swallow, her eyes light up. This will be like a date with daddy night.

John texts Erika at the Roman Spa, "Be sure you're there when I bring Taylor home." Erika is irritated that her time at the spa is cut short.

After the pharmacy, they drive to the closest ice cream shop. He requests a glass of water so his daughter can take the first pill. Then he orders two dishes of vanilla ice cream. "Daddy, this turned out to be a better day than I thought it would be. Guess what, Daddy? I really didn't feel like going to school today." John is programmed to believe whatever Erika says, so he doesn't question it. He texts Erika to be sure she's home. He explains the nurse's call and the trip to the doctors. "Would you be sure Taylor gets her medicine as directed?"

"Honey, you know I will," she reassures John.

John thanks her for helping him out. "I knew I could depend on you. You're the best!" He gives Erika and Taylor a big hug as he leaves to go back to the office.

Later in the day, Taylor and Kim discuss two books that Kim brought home from school. Taylor is teaching her little sister to read. Kim looks up to her big sister and loves sharing books with her. Whenever they read, Kim snuggles up to Taylor on the tan sofa in the family room. She tells Kim, "Doctors orders, I can't run and play but we can read." They both love to read stories.

The two sweet sisters enjoy the togetherness, they love each other. Taylor notices Kim has her shoes on the sofa. She kindly reminds her to remove them as she pulls the green plaid blanket up over their legs.

Now it's Thursday morning, the girls are already in school. Taylor is over her sore throat.

Enjoying his morning coffee, John asks Erika, "How do you think Taylor's throat is? I checked her temperature; it's back to normal. I'm relieved about that."

She tries to lessen his worry; "Taylor will be fine. Honey, your red tie with the grey stripe will look better with that grey suit. Do you have time to change it?"

"You're right, I'll go switch."

Erika pours herself a second cup before she re-ties her black robe. Two pieces of raisin bread pop up in the toaster. Sprinkling extra cinnamon-sugar on top of the buttered toast, she sets aside one for her husband. John is back, hoping for approval on the tie. She tells him, "Perfect, you are one hunk of a man!"

"What's your schedule, Honey? Would you pick up my shirts at the laundry?"

"Sure, I will have time before my hair appointment."

With John back at work, she's ready for a long, warm bath in their soaking tub. She leans back and enjoys the force of the jets as she relaxes. Forty minutes later, she dries off and gets dressed to go to Michael's Salon.

When she walks in, all three hairstylists make her feel welcome. Her stylist comments on her pastel teal sweater, "That color is very sharp on you, Erika. It complements your radiant auburn hair. You have been blessed with a wonderful shiny head of hair. You want it trimmed shoulder-length, right?" Erika nods. "Would you like a glass of wine or a cup of coffee Erika?"

Erika smirks and the stylist replies; "Silly question, huh?" A glass of chilled white wine is served. The salon is the most expensive in town, but she feels she's worth it. John is proud of the way she looks, so he'll just have to pay for it.

Erika notices the salon has had a fresh coat of paint. "Which one of you selected this color? I like it! It has a hint of pink."

The stylist remarks, "Pink walls can be horrific, but real light pink is soothing."

The haircut is finished. "It's perfect, thanks. I've never had a bad cut at this salon. That keeps me coming back. You ladies are always upbeat, I enjoy it here." She puts a generous tip in her pocket before she pays.

After she picks up her husband's shirts at the laundry, it's time to get the girls at school. While waiting in the long line of cars, she calls Nancy. It goes to voicemail. "Hi, girlfriend, it's been a while. Miss talking to you. I'm doing great; I'm living the life I always dreamed of. I go to this exquisite spa three times a week. You wouldn't believe their Thai massage. I go to the gym, shop as much as I want, get my hair and nails done whenever I want. My life would be perfect if I didn't have to deal with John's daughters and his mother. The girls drive me crazy as you know. I loathe my mother-in-law. John doesn't seem to mind all the money I spend. At least he hasn't said anything yet. I deserve it for all I have to put up with. Talk to you later."

Later that day at the law office, the secretary accepts a package from UPS. The card with it is addressed from the National Bank and reads "Congratulations for 25 years of business." Edward explains, "I forgot it was our anniversary. John, open the box." After removing the cardboard lid a special gift is revealed. The bank president is a close friend of Edwards and knows how much he loves America. Mark and John hold up the walnut framed plaque and Edward reads it aloud. The quote is from Alexander Frazier Tytler's 1790 essay. It reads:

The Life Span of a Great Civilization.

Bondage to spiritual faith,

- spiritual faith to great courage,
- courage to liberty,
- liberty to abundance,
- abundance to complacency,
- complacency to apathy,
- apathy to dependence,
- dependence back to bondage.

Edward wipes a tear from his eye. "What a great truth, Tytler had excellent insight. Let's hope America can hold onto its faith in God." John and Mark find a place to hang the special gift in the lobby.

Edward mentions, "We have had a very successful year. Our gift to charity will be increased."

John sadly responds, "I spoke with one client yesterday who lives to grow his wealth. That is sad. Just this morning I read Matthew 16:26: 'For what is a man profited, if he shall gain the whole world and lose his soul.'"

The three attorneys have a moment of reflection before returning to the conference room to work on a difficult case.

Mark comments, "I'm glad all the cases we get aren't this complicated."

Two hours later, Edward decides they need a break. "Let's go home. We'll get a fresh look at the case tomorrow. The three of us are absolutely exhausted." He closes the door and turns the key. John is hoping for a relaxing evening at home with his wife. He feels sure his daughters will be in bed.

Faking a Crisis

Little does he know Erika will be having a crisis when he gets home. A phony crisis, a self-made one. It will be timed for when he walks in the door.

In actuality, Erika has had a pleasant day. When she hears the garage door open she will work herself into a tizzy and put on an act for her husband. She will make it so convincing he will be pulled into the scenario.

She hears the garage door close. John walks in and finds her sitting at the table crying and trembling. Even though he is exhausted, he will try to comfort her. "What's wrong Erika? Tell me what happened? Your hair looks great," trying to console her as best he can.

Tears are rolling down her beautiful face; she can hardly get her breath. He has a hard time hearing her through the sobbing. "Please tell me what is bothering you."

He removes his suit coat and loosens his tie. Grabbing a Kleenex from the box on the counter, he kneels down and gently wipes her tears. Looking tenderly into her eyes, he assures her he will always be there for her. John gives her a big hug to reassure her. Erika says, "I can never go back to that salon. Your mother has caused me to look foolish. I thought she was going to be my friend and we could do things together. Boy, was I ever wrong. Your mother told the salon ladies that she is very disappointed in her new daughter-in-law. I'm devastated."

John tells her, "I'm shocked that my mother would do that, but I can see how upset you are. I'm going to have a talk with her."

She encourages John not to confront his mother. "Slow down, Honey. She probably won't remember any of it since she is getting forgetful."

John replies, "Mom has always had an astute mind. What do you mean?"

Erika continues, "She forgot the bridal appointment and went the wrong day. She forgot where she stored the briefcase on the plane. Recently, she left her house key in the door overnight. I am very worried about her. I didn't want to tell you and upset you." John finds this troubling and wonders if his father has noticed his mother's mental decline. John doesn't want to rush to any conclusions and will let the salon incident slide. So much for a relaxing evening after a difficult day at the office.

Erika loves playing the victim while pretending to protect Diane. Demeaning her mother-in-law and breaking down the trust that John has in his mother is her goal. She's clever enough not to rush things. Turning a man against his own mother isn't easy. It takes patience and time. She has plenty of both. The discussion is forgotten and John is relieved to let it go. His mind changes to thoughts of thankfulness as November approaches.

Thanksgiving

Weeks go by without an incident. It is now late November and the leaves are changing. The Carolinas are beautiful this time of year.

Taylor hollers to her sister, "Kim hurry, come up here! Daddy bought us new dresses to wear for Thanksgiving. He wants us to get ready right now. We're going to Gramma's. Hurry Kim."

"I'm coming, where are you?"

"Look in your bedroom, Kim."

She finds Taylor in front of the large free-standing dressing mirror. She is admiring herself in the soft velvety corduroy dress. Soon Kim has her new dress on. Both dresses are pastel pink with white collars and white pearl buttons. Erika tells them to wear white socks. She combs their long blonde hair and adds white barrettes.

"Go downstairs so your father can see how nice you look. We'll be leaving soon."

John is proud when he sees them. "A mother's touch is very obvious; I appreciate the little things you do for them, Erika. Okay, let's grab your mommy's homemade pumpkin pie and go." He is very impressed that Erika made the pie herself.

Meanwhile, John's parents are busy in their kitchen preparing the food. The dining room table was set the night before with the good crystal and china. A special centerpiece with yellow, rust, and orange mums is artfully arranged in a ceramic cornucopia. It stands proud in the center of the dining table. Large silver candelabras hold yellow tapers that light the table.

John, Erika, and the granddaughters have just arrived at his parent's home for a grand feast. As Taylor gets out of the car she accidently puts her left foot in the pie. She now has pumpkin on her shoe and the pie is ruined. Erika is furious with John for placing the pie on the car floor. She begins berating Taylor for her carelessness. John tries to comfort his daughter as she sobs. He is stunned to see this side of Erika. He removes Taylor's shoe and helps her up the sidewalk. "Daddy, I can hop on one foot with your help."

John's parents welcome them. Diane senses a strained atmosphere and notices that Taylor has been crying. John tells his parents that Taylor accidentally stepped in the pie. He excuses himself to clean her shoe. Taylor says, "It was an accident, Daddy." John tenderly replies, "I know that, Honey. Your feelings are more important than a pie."

The wonderful aroma causes John to peek under the lids on the covered dishes. He smells sweet potatoes with marshmallows and creamed corn casserole. He's about to tell his mother he will carve the turkey when Erika orders him into the family room. Erika is seething because John made Taylor's feelings more important than hers. Diane notices the stern look on her face. She's glad

Edward has stepped out into the garage to check out the cold drinks in their second refrigerator. He missed the bad scene Erika caused.

Diane can hear her screaming at her son. She's horrified to hear Erika disrespect John. The fact that Edward didn't hear the outburst is comforting. Just to know her son has to put up with that kind of behavior upsets her, but she can't mention it.

Edward now announces, "Dinner is on." They all gather around the lovely table and hold hands while Edward prays. It's a wonderful Thanksgiving meal. The turkey is very moist, and the stuffing has the perfect amount of sage. Most of all, everyone wants an extra serving of mashed potatoes. The two vegetables are a great addition. Diane is concerned, with everyone wanting extra mashed potatoes, will the gravy hold out?

John puts on a good face for his girls and his parents, but he doesn't know what to make of this outburst from his wife. Erika quietly simmers.

When dinner is over, the plates are removed. After an hour break, Diane serves her famous chocolate pecan pie, a southern favorite. Everyone is full and content.

After the meal, Taylor and Kim work on a puzzle on the game table. Edward and John are engrossed in a pro football game on T.V.; Erika excuses herself to call Nancy. Diane is left to do the cleanup.

Erika doesn't seem to be bothered by letting Diane do all the work. When Edward and John notice, they get busy helping out. One clears the dishes as the other loads the dishwasher. John sees Erika with her phone.

She is down the hall calling Nancy. Had John been privy to Nancy's evil nature, it simply would have been incomprehensible to him. He has no clue that his wife's friend in Albany is a very bad influence.

The phone in Albany rings five times before Nancy answers. Erika says, "Was worried you weren't home. Please assure me that I didn't mess up."

Nancy interjects, "What in the world did you do now?"

Erika goes on to explain, "Diane heard me screaming at her son, I lost control."

Nancy isn't surprised and tells her, "Don't be concerned, he will overlook anything you do. He's madly in love with you."

Nancy quickly calms her down. Erika comments, "That makes me feel better. Since Diane's such a Christian, she probably won't tell John's father. Even if she did, he would stick up for me. He was in the garage when I ripped into their son. Spending time with her is unbearable. Next, she will be planning Christmas and assume we'll spend it with them. Let her plan, we won't be there. There will be no Christmas with them. I am going to organize a surprise trip for John and the girls to Hilton Head. John will believe that I informed his mother about our trip when I didn't. This will blow up her plans and make Diane look like she is losing her mind. Knowing her, she will carefully wrap gifts, decorate the house to the hilt, and bake for days. When we don't show up, can you imagine how she will feel?"

Nancy speaks up, "Wish I could be there to enjoy it; it's genius."

Erika continues, "John has been with them every Christmas since he was born. It means a lot to him. Well, he's married to me now and things are not the same. I will have a say in things. You know me, no one plans my life. I am stubborn; he'll just have to deal with it. I am what I am. He hasn't consulted me about Christmas plans."

Their conversation ends with Erika feeling better. As she turns to go back in the family room, Erika notices a note on the bulletin board in the back hallway. Edward had penned a reminder for his wife to request a call tag from UPS. She removes the note and puts it in her pocket. Rejoining the others, Erika sees that John is ready to go home. He is thanking his parents for a wonderful time and a delicious dinner. Edward comments, "Your mother and I have enjoyed your family so very much."

Diane remarks, "I noticed Taylor and Kim enjoyed being here, they put that puzzle together. I was so busy in the kitchen; I neglected to tell them how sweet they look in their new dresses.

Just then the girls run in, "Gramma we had fun. Will you leave the puzzle on the game table? We worked hard on it." Diane assures them it can stay. After they leave, the Barringer's are ready to put their feet up. They are exhausted, but it was worth it for their family. Edward comments on what a nice day it was, Diane agrees.

John and Erika are headed home. It's quiet in the Mercedes except for the girls' chatter in the back seat. John is still processing Erika's angry outburst, but he will not let it spoil the holidays.

Christmas on Her Mind

The day after Thanksgiving every year, Diane gets busy decorating their large stately Georgian home for Christmas. After a hot cup of coffee, she is motivated to start the three-day long process. She goes into the attic and brings down boxes of Christmas decorations. Each year it is a joy to reminisce over the ornaments collected through the years. She carefully decks out the whole house. A large pine wreath with a bright red velvet bow is hung on the front door. The fifteen windows that face the street each have green pine wreaths with red bows. Both fireplace mantels are dressed with pine and red glass bulbs. There are two Christmas trees to decorate with sentimental ornaments and tiny white lights. All rooms have a touch of red and green, even the bathrooms. Their dog, Lucy, has been to the groomers. There are two red velvet bows on the Old English Sheepdog, one on each ear. Bathed and brushed, Lucy is fluffy. The dog shampoo smells so good. The curved staircase has a fresh poinsettia on each step. The iron hand railing has a garland of pine with red Christmas balls, artificial fruit, large pinecones, and magnificent tartan bows. Their grand piano has an elegant candelabra with three tall red tapers. At the base, Diane has placed shiny holly branches with red berries. The breakfast room has a wooden bowl of scented pinecones. The fragrance floats through the whole house. The double doors to the dining room open to show off the fabulous chandelier decorated with red bows. Red shades are placed on each brass light fixture.

When Edward arrives home and retrieves the mail, he realizes he has not yet received the UPS call tag. When he asks Diane about it, she looks puzzled. He reminds her that he had put a note on the bulletin board so she wouldn't forget it. He goes to the bulletin board and it is missing. He assumes Diane took the note and has no recollection of it. This episode along with the briefcase she forgot on the plane is starting to concern him.

Edward questions his wife about the note. She doesn't remember seeing it. He sees the disappointment on her face and quickly changes the subject. "Honey, you've done a great job decorating our home for the holidays. I'm so proud of you." He admires her creative work. "You are amazing! What's with that moose on the windowsill above the kitchen sink?" That puts a smile on his face. He loves her sense of humor.

Office Christmas Party

Diane smiles, she loves the holidays. Edward suggests, "Now that the house is all decorated, what do you think about having a party two weeks before Christmas? Let's invite the whole office to celebrate the birth of Christ." Diane agrees, "Give me a headcount." Edward tells her, "We'll include the janitorial crew. We get compliments from our clients about the cleanliness and the fresh smell of lemon polish when they finish. It's important to keep the office spotless. We value the whole team. Also, count the attorneys and spouses. He counts twenty-two. Better add four more; our accountant will want to bring his two sons. They are fine young men. I've added Taylor and Kim, they won't want to miss it. I count twenty-six." She calls and makes an appointment with the caterers.

Diane suggests to her husband, "Let's take Taylor and Kim shopping for new holiday dresses for the occasion. What do you think?" Edward smiles as he answers, "Great, it will be fun shopping with our granddaughters." Every moment they spend with their granddaughters is special.

Saturday is a perfect day to shop. The traffic is heavy as they drive to the department store. Once inside, Kim wants to push the elevator buttons. The Barringers are so proud of their granddaughters. A tall middle-aged clerk is enjoying showing different holiday dresses to the adorable young sisters. She comments on how polite and poised they are.

Two weeks later, everything is ready. Guests will be arriving in an hour. Meanwhile, John and the girls are waiting in the car for Erika to finish getting dressed. She stands in front of the full-length mirror primping. She knows that the low cut, figure-hugging, red velvet dress will show off her perfect sexy figure. She aims to outshine every female at the party, especially her mother-in-law. Erika has never admitted to herself that she is extremely jealous of Diane. John is in a hurry to get to his parents' house and fails to notice that her dress is too revealing. Finally, she's ready and in the car. The young sisters are quiet in the back seat as they head to gramma's.

Erika has concealed an empty beer can in her purse. As John and his daughters start up the sidewalk toward the door, she slyly drops the can near the mailbox. She smirks as she can picture religious Diane hearing about a beer can on the lawn with so many guests to witness it.

Taylor and Kim run ahead and ring the doorbell. The Barringers are all smiles when they open the door. Edward is famous for his bear hugs. Erika smiles as she wishes her in-laws Merry Christmas.

Diane is appalled seeing Erika's attire and finds it hard to believe that John would approve of his wife's dress. John notices the surprised expression on his mother's face and becomes acutely aware of his wife's appearance. John knows it's too late to do anything about it. He is embarrassed but has to admit to himself, Erika is one sexy woman.

Diane is very pleased when she sees Taylor and Kim wearing the long red tartan plaid dresses which they purchased for the girls. There is a fine metallic gold thread woven through the taffeta fabric. The soft black velvet jackets look stunning on the young blondes. Both girls have their long hair pulled up high and fastened with a black velvet bow. Diane rushes to grab the camera. This will be a picture she'll treasure. The girls look adorable as they smile for their picture-perfect moment.

John sees his dad bringing logs in for the fire. "Let me do that Dad. I'll be in charge of keeping both fireplaces burning so you can relax and enjoy your guests." This will give John somewhat of an escape from having to endure the lustful glances at Erika from the other men.

Next Mark and Heidi arrive. Heidi is taken by surprise when she sees Erika. "Oh my goodness, I came close to buying that same dress but it was too low cut for me."

Erika snidely responds, "You made the right decision; it wouldn't look good on you." Heidi is comfortable in her modest, dark green velvet dress.

John has both fires roaring. Mark takes a deep breath, "I love the smell of logs burning. Heidi, when is the last time you've smelled a real fire? Everyone has gas logs these days." She agrees, "I love that smell." Guests begin to arrive.

Erika walks into the kitchen when she sees her mother-in-law is alone. "I hope I'm wrong, but that looked like a beer can in the front yard near the mailbox." Diane is aghast!

Seeing others are busy, Diane rushes out to retrieve the beer can herself. In haste, she trips and falls on the brick sidewalk on the way back to the house. Edward hears her scream, he quickly runs to her aid. "Are you okay? Did you fall on your arm?" Soon they are all gathered around her. Edward tells John and Mark, "Make everyone feel welcome; I'm taking her to the emergency room. You're in charge."

An X-ray shows a sprain in her wrist. Diane returns to the party wearing a soft cast, she's thankful that it wasn't a fracture. The analgesic they gave her has taken away the pain, but has left her feeling tired. She is so disappointed that she cannot enjoy the party the way she wanted to.

By now the party is in full swing and everyone is enjoying themselves. The crowd is happy to see Diane is back. Edward makes sure that she is comfortable in the big recliner and jokes about the beer can. "I found my wife lying on the front sidewalk with an empty beer can in her hand." Edward is a tease and loves to joke. Diane is a great sport and joins in on the laughter.

The group gathers and discusses stories and vacations. Soft Christmas music is playing in the background. The food is amazing. A fancy tray of fruit, shrimp, caviar, and delicacies is served. They toast as they enjoy the Italian peach punch.

Taylor and Kim walk among the guests carrying polished silver trays. They politely offer guests chocolate peppermints wrapped in gold foil and salted almonds in silver foil cups.

Heidi makes a special effort to tell Edward, "I'm impressed with your granddaughters, they are very mature. I've noticed what graceful manners they have."

An hour later, the girls are getting sleepy. They have quietly gone into their grandpa's library to take a nap. After searching, they are found fast asleep on Edwards's black leather sofa. It's late, 1:00 in the morning.

With many thanks, the guests leave. Diane says, "I'm tired, let's blow out the candles and go to bed."

Edward agrees, "I will help with the clean-up in the morning." It was obvious, everyone enjoyed themselves. "You're a class act, Diane." He embraces her and says, "Let's call it a night."

"Edward, I love you. The party was a great success." He unplugs both Christmas trees and the exhausted couple go to bed.

The next morning John tells Erika, "The office party was great, don't you think so?"

"No question about it. I'm sorry your mother fell, but she was a good sport about it. After the trip to the emergency room, she returned in such good spirits. I admire her for that." Erika loathes complimenting her mother-in-law, but has to maintain her façade.

John comes up with the idea that perhaps Erika could go to the house and help with clean-up.

Fast thinking on her feet, Erika lies and tells John that she has a meeting to discuss plans for Kid Zone activities at church. No way was she going to subject herself to more agony today. John will never know that being around Diane is agonizing for her.

John proudly states, "My mother has always been an amazing woman in many ways, artistic and creative. Her friends consistently asked for her help when decorating their homes. Churches have solicited her talents to help re-do their sanctuaries. She once told a church that their front double doors were making the church look closed off and unfriendly. They replaced them with glass doors and their attendance skyrocketed. Another church put a royal purple carpet down and everyone talked about how gorgeous and appropriate it was for worship. She was ten years ahead of time in how she decorated our home. When I was a child, she made large lollipops for Christmas decorations out of big styrofoam disks, trimming them in red. They were unique. Years later, someone caught on to the idea and a large department store started selling them."

Erika asks John, "Tell me about the condo she bought in Bermuda."

He explains, "She purchased it 'pre-construction.' With blueprints in hand, she returned to North Carolina to design the interior. When it was completed, all of the furnishings were taken by truck to Miami, Florida. Then they were transferred into a container and shipped by boat to the island. She flew back to Bermuda to set it up.

Years earlier, she contracted a 4,000 sq. ft. house herself. She bought the property, had the trees cleared, designed the blueprints, and was the head contractor. It was a great success. It was located near Nashville,

Tennessee. She later sold that house with a profit of 70,000. I was very proud of her."

Erika tells John, "I can never live up to your mother. I'm sorry that she doesn't like me and probably never will."

John changes his tune, "I have never heard my mother say a negative word about anyone, much less be mean to someone. When you tell me how she has treated you, it's hard for me to understand. She has been hard on you. I don't know the reason for her attitude toward you, but I won't let her hurt you again."

Erika thanks him for supporting her. "No wonder her behavior surprises you, it shocks me too. When I hear you talk about your mother and how much you admire her, it concerns me. Bottom line is she does not like me, no matter how hard I try. She also has the problem of forgetfulness. Should you consider professional help for her? We want her to stay strong for the family. Some people change as they age."

John says, "Let's wait and see if things turn around, this is difficult for me."

Later that evening Mark calls, "I have the Bible study ready for Sunday. Marvin has agreed to give a brief talk. Erika and Heidi are taking care of refreshments. Our wives are very dependable. We're very blessed to have Christian wives. We were single until two gals from Tulane University arrived and stole our hearts. They're beautiful inside and out." John hasn't shared any negative events with his friend yet.

John adds, "They do more than their share, I also appreciate all you do, Mark. Last week we had three new people attend."

Mark corrects him, "Actually, there were four."

John is happy to hear this. "Really? That's great. Thanks for calling Mark. We'll see you in church."

Sunday is here and class begins. Mark is told this week that some members are out of town for the holidays. Erika and Heidi sit together in the second row. Mark announces: "Marvin Goldberg will present the message this week on *The Remnant*." As Marvin takes the podium, he is shocked to see two former Jewish friends in the back row. His family and friends have deserted him since he became a Messianic believer. John hands him the microphone. He proceeds to discuss *The Remnant*. "My people expected a *Deliverer in the Great Messiah*, not a baby in a manger. The manger seemed like a remnant. Israel missed it. That very baby was the God-man who would later die for sinners. God doesn't use the rich and powerful to fulfill His purpose. The nation of Israel can be seen as a remnant since it is smaller than New Jersey. But God favored it and God chose it to bring forth the Messiah. Satan has always tried to destroy it. The Jewish people are encouraged not to read Isaiah 53. That caused me to study that chapter. In it, I saw Jesus Christ as the Messiah. That inspired my journey toward Christianity." After hearing this, the former friends immediately stood up and walked out of the chapel.

All through the service, Erika was hoping for an opportunity to slide out. She has a new plan to further discredit John's mother and wants to set the scene.

Marvin wraps up his talk and hands the microphone back to John. After a few questions, the class is dismissed.

Where is Erika?

Now that class is over, John collects his daughters and has Taylor check the lady's room. "No Daddy, Mommy isn't in there." As they walk to the car Kim and Taylor start to skip.

"Girls, you have your good shoes on. You will get them scuffed up."

"Sorry Daddy," Taylor grabs her sister's hand as they continue to the car.

Erika is sitting in the front seat sobbing and shaking. John asks, "What is the matter, Erika? Please tell me, I'm here for you." Tears are flowing, she can barely speak. Tears are dripping on her Bible and her beautiful white dress. John's exasperated, he takes a deep breath. Taylor and Kim are wide-eyed and confused, afraid to speak. The girls notice their father is overwhelmed. They move back from the car, afraid to get too close.

Erika tells him, "I overheard two women in the ladies' room. One said, "Mrs. Barringer wishes John could have married Jennifer Davis. It was too bad the accident had to happen. I'm crushed. Can I use your handkerchief, John?" She wipes her fake tears.

John doesn't show his anger in front of his children, but he is furious with his mother. In a very brusque manner, he tells the girls to get in the car as he walks to the driver's side. Erika has never seen John this angry. She admonishes him to slow his breathing as he is hyper-ventilating, "John, calm down." She has to keep him from confronting his mother and having her lies exposed. "Be patient John, you're too angry. Your mom is getting older and you have to overlook things." John is start-ing to believe that his mother is trying to destroy their marriage.

Christmas is only a week away. John is concerned about his wife being around his mother. He doesn't need more conflict. Erika has turned his trust in his mother into doubt and skepticism. Being a man of character, he will be civil at his parents' home.

Christmas Shopping

Diane loves Christmas. For the past two months, she has gone on several shopping sprees, looking for special gifts for her family. Her family is like gold to her, she values them. She takes added interest in purchasing unique gifts for her new daughter-in-law. Just going in beautiful stores decorated with over the top Christmas décor is fun. Holiday music is in the air. It is such a happy time of year. Everyone seems to be cheerful as strangers wish each other "Merry Christmas." The only thing that rubs her the wrong way is when someone responds with "Happy Holidays."

The thought of ordering gifts on Amazon would never appeal to Diane, it wouldn't be the same. She goes out of her way to drop money in the kettle when she sees a Salvation Army volunteer ringing a bell. It's a tradition.

Later, when shopping is complete, wrapping begins. In the Barringers' basement, there is a special room to wrap, create, and be imaginative. There is a collection of wrapping paper, each carefully selected for all occasions. For Christmas there is solid red, leopard, and red tartan plaid, even a black wrapping paper with metallic gold crisscross lines. She has a generous assortment of ribbon for elaborate bows. Each present is wrapped with care and placed under the huge fresh pine tree. The tree is trimmed with tiny white lights, red ribbon, and fabulous bulbs. It looks like a tree you'd see in a magazine. Diane is a perfectionist and it shows in everything she does.

Walking into the family room Edward smiles to himself when he sees all the beautifully wrapped presents. He knows his wife enjoys all the work involved. She wouldn't have it any other way. Before he leaves for the office, he and Diane sit down in the breakfast room and enjoy a simple breakfast. He compliments her on the job she's done. She smiles when he says, "Honey, it's beginning to look a lot like Christmas." After a second cup of coffee and a slice of toast with raspberry jam, he kisses her on the cheek before he leaves. "See you later babe."

Now that the house is decked out and presents are wrapped, it's time to plan the menu. Diane gets the recipe books out and sorts through them. With a yawn, she decides the traditional menu will be best, just the yummy usual dishes. That is what the family will enjoy most. She writes the grocery list and heads to market. Shopping for the menu is completed. A young stock boy helps her load the car. She wishes him, "Merry Christmas" as she hands him a tip. "Thank you, Ma'am, bless you."

There are several dishes she will prepare the day before. Grinding the fresh cranberries and oranges in the food processor sends a pleasant aroma in the kitchen. To finish the cranberry sauce, she adds crushed pineapple. Decorated Santa cookies and gingerbread boy cookies were baked two days before. Diane lifts the glass dome and carefully arranges the cookies on the wooden base. Strawberry Jell-O salad is placed in the large stainless refrigerator to set. Jumbo shrimp will be the hors d'oeuvres; she places them in shell-shaped crystal cups. The sauce is made and refrigerated. She has all the ingredients to quickly mix the punch tomorrow.

A special cake in a Bundt pan is in the oven. The buzzer goes off, a beautiful rum cake is placed on the island. Rum glaze is ready to be poured over the warm cake. Diane wishes she could have a slice now with coffee, but resists the temptation. She sits down on the sofa to rest and quickly falls asleep. A twenty-minute power nap is what she needed.

Wild Sweater Party

It's Christmas Eve and Edward is home early. Friends have invited the Barringers to a 'Wild Christmas Sweater Party'. Diane has the kitchen cleaned up and she is ready to get dressed. The two will be wearing look-alike sweaters. There are green sequins in the shape of Christmas trees on the front of each sweater. Tiny, multi colored lights blink off and on, adorning the sweater trees.

Tonight they'll drive Diane's BMW to the party. Traveling to the other side of town they pass many houses decorated for Christmas. It is delightful to see all the different decorations. They come to their friend's house and see six cars parked nearby. Edward is pleased to see a Vermont license plate, "Look Diane, Roger and Beverly are here." As they walk up the sidewalk, Edward holds Diane's hand. He says, "No way will I let you fall." When they approach the house, they can hear laughter and voices from inside. They ring the doorbell. The whole group rushes to the door to see them. When they enter Diane hands the hostess her famous homemade fruitcake as a gift.

Seeing old friends means so much. Reminiscing about high school and college days brings about an adolescent joviality. Roger enjoys bringing up how Edward missed the extra point and lost the championship football game.

The hostess serves chips and dip, there's a large veggie-cheese platter. Small Hawaiian rolls are filled with roast beef. Edward enjoys the chocolate chip cookies and coffee. Wine is served but the Barringer's don't participate.

Now it's time for the group to vote for the best sweater. Diane and Edward win hands down. An adorable Rudolf with a lit red nose is presented to the couple. Edward turns the switch on the base. Loud and clear, "Grandma Got Run over by a Reindeer" blares out. He lets it play awhile. It's hilarious to see a room full of seniors getting a huge kick out of the song as it plays on. It's been a great evening and a wonderful Christmas Eve. Roger asks, "Where did you find that reindeer, in an antique mall?" The hostess responds, "I searched the internet." The group ends the evening before midnight. What a memorable night. The gang enjoyed seeing each other. Can Christmas with friends be topped by Christmas with family?

One Huge Disappointment

It's Christmas morning. You can smell baked ham and apple pies in the oven. Dinner rolls and pecan pies are on the kitchen counter. Salad, creamed peas, and asparagus spears are ready. Candles are lit on the table. All of the best silver and china are in place. Potatoes are ready to be mashed and gravy is on the stove. A CD is playing 'I'll be Home for Christmas' by Bing Crosby.

All of a sudden, John calls to wish his parents a Merry Christmas. Edward takes the call.

When he hears John's voice, he immediately calls out "Merry Christmas son. We are ready for you all to arrive. I can't wait to see Taylor and Kim open their gifts."

John's response cuts to the core. "Didn't mom tell you? Don't tell me she forgot. My wife said she made it very clear to mom. Erika planned a surprise trip for us; we're spending Christmas in Hilton Head. I will miss having Christmas with you and mom. Erika said she told mom about the plans two weeks ago."

"This is the first I've heard of it" replied Edward somberly. "We are all ready for your family to walk in the door. Evidently, your mother's memory is declining. Now I have to tell her your family won't be joining us. She has gone to so much work getting ready. Your mother is going to be devastated and so disappointed, I am as well."

John says, "I feel bad."

Edward is distraught, "You feel bad? How do you think your mother is going to feel?"

John answers, "We're almost there, we left early this morning. Erika's driving, seeing the road signs I finally realized where we are headed. She has our car trunk packed with suitcases and presents. She told me about a 30-foot Christmas tree in the lobby and the concert grand piano which has a fabulous pianist. Hotel guests all gather around to sing carols. Erika wanted the girls to experience all of this. I hear the dinner there is out of this world. Dad, I couldn't disappoint Erika. I had no idea that you didn't know. I'm worried about Mom's memory."

Edward says, "We will make the best of it John, enjoy your day. Love you, Son." They hang up with no hard feelings.

Edward's heart sinks, he dreads telling his wife. In his mind, he blames Diane's deteriorating memory, but he would never mention it to her. Should he consider getting her professional help? That itself would hurt her. The very thought that the family thinks she's losing it would destroy her.

There is no way to tell Diane without hurting her. He wishes there was. He walks slowly to the kitchen wondering how to say it. He starts, "That call was John. Erika made plans for their family to have Christmas at a resort in Hilton Head. They are almost there. John said that Erika told you about her plans weeks ago."

Diane's shocked. "Tell me you're joking."

Edward assures his wife, "It's no joke." There's a long silence, Diane's eyes fill with tears. Edward hugs her tight; they can't speak for a few minutes.

Diane contemplates it. "Really? I suppose she might have, but I certainly can't recall such a conversation. I don't think that I would forget something as important as that. We will have to make the best of a bad situation. How do we do it?"

Edward then comes up with a great idea.

Holiday with the Homeless

"We will call the homeless shelter and invite them all to our dinner table."

"Oh Edward, you're a genius. You know the manager of the shelter, don't you? Call now and see if we can make it happen."

The call goes through and the man on the other end listens to their request. He will call back in ten minutes. A moment later, the call comes in. "Can you handle ten guests?" Edward says, "Perfect, our table seats twelve. My wife and I want to have Christmas dinner with them."

Shortly, a small crowd with big smiles on their faces shows up at the door. Edward and Diane are so happy. She says, "What a wonderful Christmas." Their guests are wide-eyed as they enter the mansion so beautifully and warmly embellished. One of the ladies says, "This is going to be the best Christmas I've ever had." They can smell the delicious food and hear the wood crackling from the two large fireplaces.

The group includes four women and six men. One lady is in awe, "I've never been in a house like this. It is so big and pretty." The Barringer's are gregarious as they welcome their guests. Edward ushers them in, Diane leads them to the dining room. They take their seats.

Edward says a prayer of thanks for the Savior, the food and their guests.

The food is served. They waste no time digging into the delicious dishes. Diane gets many compliments. Most of the guests want seconds. The men request extra ham and mashed potatoes, the women favor the Jell-O salad.

Edward and Diane engage each one in conversation, asking them about their lives, their hopes, and dreams. They are open to sharing their experiences. The guests are surprised to find that someone cares enough to ask and listen.

All are full and content. The dishes are cleared and dessert is served. Diane pours them coffee. The rum cake is the favorite choice, but one woman wants apple pie.

They are invited into the large family room to sit around the warm fire. Diane asks if anyone would like hot chocolate. Most were too full from dinner but a couple of men said they would like a cup. Diane adds a marshmallow on top for a special touch.

Edward opens his Bible to read about the birth of Christ from the book of Luke. He explains how God sent His only Son to the earth to live a perfect life. He kept all of the Ten Commandments and was without sin. He explained how God requires perfection and sinlessness because he is a holy and righteous God. Edward quotes Romans 3:23, "We have all sinned and fallen short of the glory of God." We cannot go to heaven when we die until our sin has been removed. Jesus did this for sinners by taking their sins upon Himself and then dying for them on the cross. He took the wrath of God upon Himself to save sinners. He arose from the dead on the third day and now sits in heaven, next to the Father. He intercedes for us. They listen intently, and Edward tells them that to be saved from their sin, they need to ask the Lord Jesus to forgive them of their sins. Turn away from sin and live for Him. He closes with a heartfelt prayer for each of them and gives thanks for the Savior, in Jesus's name, Amen.

A young man in the group said, "Sir, that is so kind of you and your wife, I feel like I'm dreaming. This can't be real, somebody pinch me!"

"You're not dreaming," Edward comments. "You're a delightful group."

It's been two and a half hours. A call comes in, the van will be here in thirty minutes to take them back to the shelter. The guests thank the Barringer's for the dinner before leaving. One middle-aged man says to Edward, "I feel hopeful for the first time in many years." Edward gives him the phone number to reach him in case he wants to talk.

When the driver arrives, he sees the broad smiles on their faces. As the van pulls away, Mrs. Barringer puts her arm around Edward's waist and says, "It turned out to be the most blessed Christmas we have ever had."

Two days later they receive a text, John's family is home from Hilton Head. They spent Christmas at the Grande Ocean resort. Taylor and Kim enjoyed the experience, but John has been sad because he had to disappoint his parents. Erika is proud of herself for ruining

Diane's plans. Little does she know that by God's grace, her in-laws turned it into something wonderful.

Edward texts back, "Hope your Christmas went well, our's ended up great! Your mom and I made the day count. It worked out well; tell you more about it later."

John replies, "Kim and Taylor are sleepy, I'm putting them to bed." John unloads their car, presents and suitcases are taken in. Erika unpacks the suitcases; things are put back in their places. Clothes go in the laundry; she starts up a load of whites. After getting a handle on unpacking, she enters the master bath and closes the door.

Making sure she's alone, she calls Nancy.

Connecting with Nancy

Nancy notices that Erika's name came up on her phone. She answers, "How did your holiday plans work out? Was your mother-in-law devastated?" Erika answers, "I hope she was furious. John believes that I told his mother two weeks prior to Christmas that we wouldn't be there. They all think she is losing her mind. I have a gift for her."

Nancy is curious, "What are you giving her?"

She responds, "I heard that Diane is deathly afraid of spiders. There is a new age shop in the mall. I found a pin in the image of a black widow spider, it looks so real. I wrapped it in silver paper and added a red bow."

Nancy comments, "I love it. Wish I could see her face when she opens it.

Erika responds, "I will give it to her at the right time. No way do I want to see her open it." Nancy comments, "Has she figured out yet that you don't like her?" Erika says, "This will be the most blatant thing I've done to her. Usually it's more subtle but she hasn't connected the dots."

Nancy remarks, "Nothing you do, Erika, surprises me. I'm sure you didn't tell John about the gift." Erika reassures her, "Are you crazy? He knows very little of what I do. I have to hang up, he's home."

John walks in with a troubled look on his face, "Erika, I realize the relationship with you and my mother is not ideal. I'm convinced it's all her fault. Not only is her memory slipping, she refuses to accept you. She doesn't give you a chance."

The Cruise

Each day on his way to the office John tunes into BNN, a Christian Radio station. Today his ears perk up. They are announcing a Christian Cruise. There will be special speakers and awesome gospel singers. Excited, he dials up Erika and tells her all about it. He mentions that his mom would love it and it would be a chance for the two of them to bond. She's all for it, "John, it will be good for your mom to get to know me better."

He tells her, "I'll call my mother and take care of all the details, even a babysitter." He's feeling encouraged.

Diane is excited to go on the cruise and is hopeful that things will be improved with her daughter-in-law. Vacationing in the West Indies sounds so appealing, as does shopping during the day on various islands. Good food, great gospel music, and evangelical speakers all sound wonderful. John and Edward are both for it.

Erika gets Nancy on the phone and a sinister discussion follows. Nancy tells her, "This could be a great opportunity. Just because there's a bunch of Christians on a boat, that doesn't mean an accident can't happen. You'll have to cause it. Very often, the decks on these large ships are slippery. Knowing you Erika, you'll get the job done. I'm eager to hear the results."

Diane is all for the cruise until she talks to Grace. "Diane I'm sorry, I've heard that there have been accidents on cruises, more people fall overboard than you realize. Please don't go."

Diane says, "Oh Grace, I've been looking forward to going. I am disappointed that you don't feel I should." She trusts Grace and has to admit to herself that her friend is always right.

That evening, Diane calls Erika to tell her she won't be going. No reason is given. Erika tells her how disappointed John will be. After the cruise is canceled, she wonders if an opportunity to bond with her daughter-in-law has been missed. John worked hard organizing it.

Diane hated to disappoint Edward and John. How could a BNN cruise be anything but wonderful? Maybe Grace is wrong, she might be over-protective. Yet on the other hand, what if she's right? Grace has always had good instincts, why second-guess now? She decides to let it go and stop questioning her decision. She will be content and stay home.

Erika is also very disappointed, but for a different reason. Her reason is sinister and now she has to explain this to her evil friend.

She calls Nancy, who asks, "Are you going to pull this off? If a body is lost at sea no one can prove how it happened. It's a perfect plan."

"Calm down, Nancy. Diane canceled."

Nancy asks, "Oh, crap! What happened?"

"Her friend talked her out of it. Edward and John thought it was a great idea, they want the family united. They wanted Diane and me to bond."

Nancy tells Erika, "Don't worry, you'll come up with another plan. Call me when you do." They both hang up disappointed.

That evening John's family drops in unexpectedly at his parents. He wants to talk to his dad about something concerning the office. The canceled cruise is briefly mentioned. Edward says, "There will be many opportunities for other cruise vacations. We are happy you decided to stop by and visit with us tonight." They hug Taylor and Kim. It is a short visit; the girls are tired. They sit and talk awhile.

On the way home, John thanks Erika for being so nice to his mother after all the wrong she's done. "I admire you for being above it all."

Erika asks, "Did you hear me ask your mom to go to lunch tomorrow?"

John is surprised, "No I didn't, is she going?" Erika answered, "Yes, she seemed willing to go. I'm meeting her at 12:30 at Paris Place. I'm looking forward to it, hoping it goes well." John shakes his head. "You amaze me, Erika, I'm proud of you."

Paris Place is a cozy little restaurant. Soft pink walls are a nice backdrop for the sparkling crystal chandeliers. White wrought iron tables and chairs are neatly arranged on the polished pine floors. Pink tablecloths and napkins add to the charm. Each table has a potted pink geranium. On the long wall is an ornate, white antique fireplace. A large painting over the mantel repeats pink geraniums in a still life, setting the tone. Classical music is playing softly. The young perky waitresses are dressed in white with crisp black aprons. On the bibs of the aprons, "Paris Place" is embroidered in heavy pink thread.

When Diane and Erika walk in, the hostess compliments Diane on her beautiful navy suit. She thanks her.

Diane has no idea Erika has been building a case against her. The conversation is pleasant, mostly about the granddaughters. A young blond waitress walks over to take their order. Erika says, "Let's order sweet potato fries for starters."

Diane suggests they share the turkey melt with avocado. "Doesn't that sound delicious?" They agree, and the order is placed.

Trying to maintain a positive mood, Diane compliments Erika, "I've heard how hard you work at the hospital. You are also taking good care of Taylor and Kim." They spend some time discussing local news. As they visit, Erika is somewhat uneasy. She folds her napkin and refolds it two or three times. Diane doesn't read anything into it. It's a habit Erika does when she's nervous. A thought comes to her, what if Diane shows John the gift? Oh well, I'll just deny it.

The lunch comes to a close and it's time for Erika to pick-up the girls at school. Diane gets the tab; they walk out together to the parking lot. She tells her mother-in-law, "Thanks for lunch, I enjoyed being with you." She hands Diane the Christmas gift as they walk to their cars. Diane is relaxed and has no idea what is next.

Diane wastes no time opening the gift once she's in her car. She lets out a scream and quickly puts the lid back on the box when she sees the spider pin. It sends chills up her spine. It is so real looking. It's about three inches in size with tiny rhinestone eyes. She is deathly afraid of spiders. Why did Erika give her such a spiteful gift? It must have been a joke. No, it was just plain mean! Diane keeps the disturbing gift a secret. She doesn't want to share it or think about it. Why would her daughter-in-law do that? It makes no sense to her. It was cruel. It reminds Diane of another mean gift Erika had given her. When she opened that present she was thrilled to see an elegant Lalique perfume bottle. Her first thought was how wonderful the beautiful bottle would look on her dressing table. She carefully removed the crystal stopper and held it close to her nose. Her eyes began to water and burn. The terrible smell was Clorox. Even then, Diane kept the malicious present to herself. Realizing Erika's anger runs deep, Diane decides that the best thing she can do is pray for her troubled daughter-in-law.

Later that afternoon, John calls Erika to see how it went. "Did you make any headway with mom?"

Erika tells him, "She set me straight, blood is thicker than water. You will always put her first."

John is shocked, "Good grief, has she lost her mind? I wonder if Dad notices any odd behavior."

Erika says, "Slow down, don't involve your father. You know he has a pacemaker. Don't worry, I'll just overlook what she said. I'm a big girl. She is slipping, some of the things she forgets don't add up. When we finished our lunch, I remarked about picking up the girls at school. Her answer was, "What school?" She wasn't making any sense. She forgot the girls go to school, I was shocked, but I didn't respond. She even forgot the name of the school." John is concerned.

When the weekend comes, he calls to invite his parents over for lunch, "Hi Dad. I'm going to cook burgers on the grill. Can you and mom come over?" Edward accepts, he's sure Diane will be glad to come too.

John has always had a close relationship with his parents. Inviting them over seems like a normal thing to do. Erika gets home and enters the kitchen. He tells her, "I've invited my parents for lunch."

"You did what? We have no food ready. John, you should always check with me. I might be tired. I'm not in the mood for guests. You never consult me!" She's really upset that he didn't get her permission; this could mean trouble for her.

"I apologize. I should have discussed it with you first. We must be more informed on mother's problem before we get professional help. I plan to have a conversation with her to check her memory. Remember how she couldn't recall if her granddaughters went to school or where? There are questions I need answered. Without assessing her memory, we can't make assumptions." What if John asks his mother the wrong questions? This silently worries Erika.

Erika is angry and feels once again John is putting someone else's welfare above her own. She stomps out of the room and slams the door. She's worried he won't see any problem with Diane. Will he realize his wife is making it all up? She will stay close to control things.

John goes to a local deli to buy potato salad, then stops at the bakery for his dad's favorite key lime pie.

Taylor and Kim carry out the plastic patio dishes and forks, they neatly place the orange and turquoise dishes on the table. Kim brings out the condiments and plastic glasses.

Soon their grandparents arrive. When they step out of Edward's white jeep, Taylor and Kim run over to hug them. Erika walks out and welcomes her in-laws, she has no choice.

Eating outside is always fun for the girls. Kim asks, "Can we sit by you when we eat Gramma?"

"Of course you can, I would be honored."

Taylor says, "Oh good, we love it when you visit. Can I sit by you too, Gramma?"

When John returns from the bakery, he notices his wife and mother are having a serious conversation. He is confident Erika can handle it.

Soon Edward is busy flipping the burgers; he has green peppers and onions sautéing in a small skillet on the grill. Edward hollers, "John, can you smell these onions? They smell so good! Where are the buns?"

"I'm toasting the buns. Call everyone, we're ready to eat."

The family gathers, and Edward offers thanks before they sit down. Diane has a granddaughter seated on each side of her. The girls are very talkative, they're little chatterboxes.

Taylor notices, "Gramma and Mommy both have orange tee shirts on, only Gramma's has long sleeves."

Erika speaks up, "Mine is orange and white check."

Kim says, "You both have white pants on."

John reminds them, "Girls, do more eating and less talking. Please pass the potato salad, anyone want seconds?"

Erika compliments Edward, "The burgers are done perfectly."

Taylor asks, "May Kim and I be excused?"

Edward calls out, "Who wants key lime pie?"

The girls aren't interested in having pie, and they are excused. They race over to the swing set. The sky is starting to look gray but not concerning.

The Tornado

An hour later, the sky turns darker. Kim runs up to Diane, "Gramma, look at that big black cloud."

Edward is concerned, "Turn on the weather channel."

The local news announces a tornado is imminent, take cover. All hands-on deck; the family pulls together for cleanup. John says, "Dad, do you think we should all go over to your place?"

Edward agrees, "We have the second kitchen in the lower level, we keep it stocked."

Diane adds, "Also, we have a generator."

As they all get set to leave, Erika goes in the house. John is looking for her. Taylor says, "She's in the bathroom."

After rubbing pink rouge on her arms, she calmly walks out and rejoins the family. Acting nonchalant, she wants her husband to notice as she pretends to scratch her arms. Edward warns, "I checked my phone again, the tornado is moving fast. It took a sudden turn toward Mooresville. Let's get a move on it."

Erika balks as John takes her aside, "What's wrong? We'll be safer there."

"Look, I get hives when I'm stressed. It hasn't happened to me in many years. My arms are itching. Being near your mother is taking a toll on me. Why do you put me through this?"

John holds out her arms and sees the redness, "I'm sorry Erika." She begins to scratch again.

"Your mother shared a lot with me earlier, I can't handle all of this negativity. You have no idea how confused she is. Please don't ask me to rehash it with you. Hearing it twice, Oh, I can't take it. From now on, I don't want to be around your mother."

Just then, Taylor feels raindrops. She asks, "Daddy, could lots of rain cause a flood? My Sunday School teacher told us about Noah's flood."

Edward interjects with a laugh, "There wasn't any global warming back then."

"Grampa, are you being silly?"

John interrupts, "Yes Taylor, your grampa is making fun of global warming. Dad, the rain is starting to come down hard. Please take the girls to your house now. We'll be over soon."

Erika becomes defiant. She takes a deep breath, pretending to relieve her anxiety. John realizes the difficulty his mother has caused. Erika can barely stand to be in her presence. He's in a dilemma but will protect his wife. He tries to persuade his wife, "It's a storm and we have to go where it's safe."

Before John and Erika have a chance to reconsider and leave, the weather turns for the worse. Now it's too late to go. A large gust of wind rips off part of the roof on the front porch. The neighbor's tree falls with a crash across their driveway. They are both frightened when they see the predicament they're in. John tries to comfort his wife, "Erika we are blessed, we are both okay. It's a good thing my parents took the girls with them."

Erika says, "Hold me, this is frightening."

John comforts her. "I will protect you. We will get all the damage repaired and the tree removed."

The pounding rain has let up and the powerful winds have slowed. The fierce storm was fast moving.

An hour later the sun comes out. The white jeep pulls up, the girls are home. Edward calls Diane to explain the damage done at John's house.

"I'll stay and help clean up."

A call is made to professionals to do the heavy work and roof repairs.

Edward inserts, "What are we doing wrong? Seems like God is testing us as he tested Job. The hotel fire, Diane's fall and now this."

Erika offers her opinion, "Perhaps we are being chastised for one person's sin. Oh, I'm shocked that I actually said that." Immediately she puts her hand over her mouth. "This is a very godly family, I misspoke. Forgive me."

Edward says, "We know you didn't mean how it sounded. However, God does test those he loves. Will His people turn against Him when things go poorly, or will they push through the trial with grace? Life is full of choices. God is in control no matter what happens. Bad times or good times, we are to be thankful."

John is relieved. Three days later the porch roof is repaired, the neighbor's tree is removed, and things are back to normal. This has been a storm to remember.

John brings up his mother again, "Erika, I didn't notice any change in mom's mental health, but I believe you. You have spent more time around her lately than I have. We must seek out the very best psychologist for her. In the meantime, I will protect you. Try to stay away from her until we know more."

John found Dr. Joseph Rossi, a board-certified neuropsychologist in Charlotte with a 5-star rating. He calls and makes an appointment for his mother. Working up the courage to tell his mother won't be easy. He anticipates that his dad will be relieved, but his mother will insist there is nothing wrong with herself.

Two days later, Erika tells John that Dr. Rossi's office called and canceled the appointment because he is backlogged with patients. She convinces John to wait a little longer. John values her opinion and waits. In truth, Erika cancelled the appointment. She couldn't risk the doctor claiming that Diane was in good psychological health.

Erika feels very confident and wants to talk with her friend. Taylor is increasingly irritating her now. Nancy knew this would happen sooner or later. Erika has a few minutes to spare, she dials up Nancy.

Nancy picks up. Erika blares out, "This is so easy. John has complete confidence in me. Now I have to step up the game and get him completely away from his mother. I plan to turn Taylor and Kim against her too. One step at a time."

Nancy asks, "How are you doing with his children?"

"I'm okay with Kim but the oldest one, I just hate that child. She looks like and acts like Diane. She is a brat! I am mean to her, but she deserves it. Nancy, John would be furious if he heard me say that. I'm glad I have you for a sounding board."

As evil as Nancy is, she has a soft spot when it comes to children. She settles Erika down.

"This isn't about his children; it's about getting even with his mother."

Erika respects her friend, but decides to end the call. She hates being corrected. "I will do what I want concerning my stepchildren."

Kim and Taylor's Birthdays

Spring is here, it comes early in the Carolinas. Kim and Taylor are discussing their birthdays and that they were both born in the same month.

Taylor asks, "Kim, how will we celebrate?"

Kim answers her sister, "Let's get mommy to bake pretty cupcakes. We can take them to school and hand them out to our friends."

Taylor likes the idea.

Kim says, "Mommy, for my birthday tomorrow will you make cupcakes for my class?"

Erika smiles and says, "I'll be glad to, Honey. Let's frost them in pink and put sprinkles on them."

Kim is thrilled, "I love that idea. Taylor's birthday is in five days after mine. Let's make cupcakes for her next week."

Erika says, "We'll see. It is your birthday we're baking for first." She can't help herself, she is jealous of Taylor. She hasn't decided yet if she'll even bake cupcakes for Taylor. Tomorrow Erika will take special care decorating Kim's cupcakes.

It's getting close to bedtime. Taylor gets out her favorite book, "Don't Let the Pigeon Drive the Bus." The cute young blondes are snuggled under a navy-blue blanket as Erika finishes up the story. They giggle and giggle with glee.

When the story is over, Erika calls to the girls, "Hot Cocoa anyone?" Excited, they run to the kitchen table. Erika grabs two cups and fills them with milk and cocoa mix. Kim's is out of the microwave first.

"Thanks Mommy, this is so yummy." She licks her lips.

Next Taylor gets hers and takes a big sip, "Ouch! I burnt my tongue, mine is way too hot. My tongue is so sore. It hurts bad."

Erika yells, "Don't be such a baby. Blow on it, it will cool down."

She is unconcerned with Taylor's cries, "Quick girls, finish your cocoa. Now run upstairs and jump into bed." After they grab their teddy bears and say a short prayer, Erika tucks Kim into bed. Taylor is left to pull up her own blanket. "Rosebud, please snuggle up with me. I need a hug from my teddy bear."

The next morning Kim wakes up early. She runs to the window and opens the blinds, "Yippee, it's a perfect day."

The sun is streaming in her window. Kim is very excited, now she'll decide what adorable outfit will look the best for this special day. She climbs up on a step stool in her closet. There are lots of outfits to choose from. Thinking out loud she says, "Yellow! I will wear this cute little yellow outfit. Oh yes. I'll find my yellow socks, the ones with ruffles. Then I'll wear my white sandals."

Being young, Kim has picked up on some bad traits of her stepmom's style and ego.

She combs her long blonde hair; the full-length mirror reflects a pleased smile. She runs downstairs to get approval from her mother. Erika tells her, "You look adorable, Honey. We'll be leaving as soon as Taylor comes downstairs."

A moment later, her big sister bounds down the stairs, jumping over the last step and landing on her feet. Taylor's all smiles. She tucks in her white tee shirt and grabs her backpack.

The girls pile in Erika's Nissan, backpacks and all. Taylor's arms are swinging like a music director as she sings, "Happy Birthday to Kim, happy birthday to my little sister." Taylor loves Kim. The girls are in a great mood as Erika drives them to school. Taylor goes to her class. Erika walks Kim to her classroom. Mrs. Norris notices Kim is especially excited today. She remembers it's her birthday. Erika lets her know she'll be back at 2:30 with cupcakes for everyone.

A chubby little boy in the front row hollers out "Alright!" as he rubs his hands together. The whole class is anxious for a cupcake.

A little girl in the third row raises her hand and blares out, "I hope they are chocolate!"

It's now two-thirty and Erika knocks on the class-room door. Mrs. Norris opens it. "Look class, Kim's mother has brought a tray full of delicious cupcakes. Kim is five years old today; let's all sing "Happy Birthday." Soon Kim is handing each one a pink cupcake. When she finishes, she licks frosting off her fingers and goes to her seat. Kim thanks Mrs. Norris and her mom. She is very proud and happy.

Soon the bell rings and school is out. Erika picks up the empty tray then she and Kim go down the hall to get Taylor. Taylor is eager to see if there's a cupcake left for her. Erika says, "There was one left but I gave it to the janitor. Sorry, I should have saved it for you." Taylor has a sad look on her face, but does not comment. A small tinge of rejection touches her heart, she's very disappointed.

At home, John is waiting to celebrate. He's especially cheerful as he welcomes his family at the door. "Happy Birthday, Kim! Gramma and grampa are here. Gramma has made your favorite dinner, shepherd's pie." Edward leads Kim to the table to see the pretty white frosted cake. 'Happy Birthday Kim' is scrolled across the top in blue frosting.

When dinner is over Kim thanks her, "Thanks Gramma that was the best ever shepherd's pie." Her cake has five candles; Erika lights them. Kim easily blows them all out. Her wish is for a new bike. Almost like magic it suddenly appears. It is bright purple with training wheels, purple and pink streamers dangle from each handlebar. Kim screams with joy, "I love it! Thank you, thank you!"

Taylor likes to see her little sister happy.

The new bike has Kim so excited she almost forgets to open the gift from her grandparents. Taylor hands her the present wrapped in yellow and silver striped paper with a matching fluffy bow. Kim anxiously rips open the present to find an elegant jewelry box. Her eyes widen as she lifts the lid to see a petite china doll in a pink dress twirling to the music. Kim asks, "Gramma, what song is playing?"

Diane informs her, "The Blue Danube Waltz," Honey. I had a similar musical jewelry box when I was young. I'm glad you like it." Kim carefully places the special box on the dining room buffet then rushes back to examine her new bike.

Taylor runs into the laundry room and pulls a green step stool under the calendar. "Look Daddy, now I can reach the calendar. Each morning for the next five days, I'll climb up and check off a day. I can't wait for my birthday."

John gives his little girl a big hug. Taylor asks her dad, "May I have a puppy for my birthday?"

Erika hears her request and yells, "No dogs, I'm allergic and I'll get sick!"

He has to say, "No, I'm sorry, Honey."

Taylor's sad, she already had a name picked out for her puppy, "That's okay Daddy, we don't want mommy to get sick."

John is amazed at how well she handled the disappointment. The next few days go by quickly. It's now Taylor's 7th birthday.

Finally it's here, Taylor is excited. She asks her mom, "Will you please bring pretty pink cupcakes to school today for me? Can I have sprinkles?"

Erika firmly says, "Finish your cereal and drink your orange juice. It's time to go to school."

"I'm so happy. My birthday will be fun even if I don't get a puppy. I will give each of my friends a cupcake," exclaims Taylor.

Erika replies, "Girls, are you ready to go? Taylor, you let me worry about the cupcakes." Erika rushes the girls into the car. "Hurry, so you won't be late."

The girls run to their classes. Taylor walks into her room all smiles. She says, "Ms. Reed, do you know what today is?"

Her teacher answers, "No sweetheart, what day is it?"

"It's my birthday and my mom is going to bring pink cupcakes for the whole class."

Ms. Reed says, "That will be wonderful! Taylor, we will celebrate your birthday." Ms. Reed can't help but notice that Taylor, who is always happy, is extra exuberant today. Her eyes have a special sparkle.

As the day goes on, Taylor keeps watching the clock. She skips to the front of the room and asks, "Ms. Reed, what time do you think she'll bring the cupcakes?" The teacher tells her 2:30. It's only 2:00. Taylor has a fear of being disappointed.

Meanwhile, Erika is home watching a movie on TV. No cupcakes have been made. The cake mix is on the island unopened. Erika enjoys disappointing Taylor.

Taylor is still watching the clock. It's 3:30 and Erika isn't there yet. Mrs. Reed has the class sing happy birthday. Taylor's smile is gone, her heart is broken. Ms. Reed feels terrible; Taylor is such a special little girl. She gives her a big hug. Tears are running down her cheeks and dripping on her light blue T-shirt.

School has been dismissed, Erika walks in ten minutes late saying, "Sorry, my day was so hectic, I didn't make the cupcakes." Taylor has a lump in her throat. It was so important to her and she is feeling deeply hurt.

Erika and Kim head for the car, Taylor lags behind. She wipes her warm tears on her sleeve. When she finally gets in the Nissan, she slumps in the backseat. Overcome with sadness, nothing else seems to matter. Her stepmother doesn't care. What Taylor needs is a hug from Erika, so she can feel loved. Taylor is too young and innocent to comprehend an adult who hates and has no love to give.

Erika speaks out harshly, "The world doesn't revolve around you, Taylor. We are almost home. Don't let your father see you crying; don't cause trouble for me."

Erika explains to John, "What a hectic day I've had. I just couldn't find time to bake."

John believes his wife and is sure her day was difficult. He sees such sadness in his daughter's face. He came home early to wish her a happy birthday. He says, "Let's all go out to dinner. Your gramma and grampa can join us."

Shortly, the Barringers arrive. Diane hands Taylor a beautifully wrapped pink gift with a polka dot bow. She carefully unwraps a pink backpack with blue hearts. "Wow, this is great! It even has an extra pocket with Velcro. Thank you so much. How did you know my old backpack had a rip in it?" Taylor hugs her grandparents when she thanks them.

John announces, "We are all going to the Catawba Golf Club for dinner to celebrate Taylor's birthday." It's a short drive to the country club. The law firm has memberships there for all the attorneys and their families to enjoy.

They are about to leave when Taylor runs upstairs to her room. Tossing the pillows off her bed in search of her friend. "There it is!" Taylor grabs her white cuddly bear, Rosebud.

John has requested the family be seated at one of the glass top tables on the terrace. The surrounding flower gardens are perfectly manicured. The hostess lights the large white candle in the center of the table. John has requested seven pink balloons with helium to be tied to his little princess's chair. Taylor is all aglow. Rosebud is perched in front of her on the table. They order her favorite, Lobster and Shrimp Primavera with Alfredo Sauce. The delicious meal is enjoyed by all.

After dinner, the whole staff brings a pink frosted cake in and sings "Happy Birthday." Taylor blows all seven candles out as she makes a wish. John notices that Taylor has tears welling up in her eyes and believes they are tears of joy.

Kim begs her sister to tell her the wish. Taylor says, "No Kim, it's a secret."

Holding Rosebud close, she whispers in her teddy bear's ear. "I wish Mommy could love me." She wipes her tears on her napkin.

Before the family goes home, Taylor thanks the waitresses for the cake. "Thank you a million times. How did you get all of those strawberries inside my cake?"

She answers, "It's magic, it only happens for special little girls."

Taylor feels special tonight, and Kim is happy for her.

When they arrive home, John wheels out a beautiful pink bike. It has a white basket on the handlebars with pink flowers. Taylor puts Rosebud in the basket and thinks it's a good fit. "Daddy, I will be able to take her for rides with me." Taylor has a big smile on her face, "Kim and I can go for bike rides together." Taylor is happy as she jumps into bed and cuddles with Rosebud.

Now with the girls in bed and John's parents' home, Erika wants to look good for her husband, "I felt so bad that I couldn't find time to bake for Taylor. Thanks to you it turned out fine, she deserved a special birthday." By now it's 9:00 and John decides to watch a documentary on Channel 3. The program doesn't interest Erika.

She takes the liberty to walk around the house to see what changes will make it feel more like her home. She wants to paint rooms and replace some lamps and bed covers. She walks outside and decides there should be a pergola in the back yard and a swing on the front porch. She plans to have the picket fence repaired and painted. It's old and falling apart, but she loves the fence. She feels sure when repaired it will add ambiance to the house. When John's program on TV is over, they call it a night and go to bed.

John's glad the weekend's here. When he pulled into the driveway yesterday, he decided to take down the old fence. Now that it's Saturday, he has planned to tackle the job. Erika is sleeping in; he has no idea that she has a different plan.

He gets up early and goes to the garage. Selecting the right tools for the job, he rolls up his red plaid shirt sleeves and gets to work. With a sledgehammer, he attacks the fence. Even though he isn't used to manual labor, he breaks off large sections. The fence posts are set in concrete and are very hard to remove. The nails and screws are taken out and the wooden slats are piled on the curb. Soon there is a large pile of broken fence by the road. He is sure Erika will be proud of the new clean look in the front yard.

Now he's ready to clean up and go in for a hot cup of coffee. Erika is just waking up. Being sure she'll be very proud of the job he's done, he shows her the results. Erika verbally explodes! Shrieking like a maniac, "Why didn't you ask me what I wanted done with the fence? I wanted it repaired and painted. I'm furious! I hope you're happy." John takes a deep breath. Amy was never this complicated and hard to please.

Again, he is shocked to see such a temper. She's still screaming. He is embarrassed and feels sure that the neighbors can hear her. John is shocked to realize what a violent temper she has. He loves Erika and attributes her behavior to her childhood. However, he is concerned about how it might affect his young daughters. This outburst of anger is the worst he has seen. He watches as she goes back in the house, slamming the door behind her. He stands there frozen in shock.

John gives Mark a call. He tells him about the fence he removed. He's hesitant to tell Mark about Erika's outbursts of anger but has no one else to talk to. Mark is his best friend and will have good advice. He tells Mark, "I need to talk to you about a personal matter." They set a future time to talk. Hoping she'll heal from her anger, John often prays for his wife. He wonders if tomorrow on the plane would be a good time to ask Mark for advice.

Early the next morning, John rushes to the airport. Mark is waiting at the departure gate. They leave for a long-planned business trip. For the first time, he is concerned about the girls being with Erika. He asked his parents to stop in and check on them without giving Erika a notice.

During the flight, John confides in Mark about Erika's irrational behavior. Mark lets him know that Heidi had told him about Erika's abusive childhood. He suggests that John track down her mother and visit her. Perhaps an encounter with her would answer his many questions. John is determined to do that as soon as possible. He loves his wife and wants her to heal.

Later that day Erika drives the girls home from school. Kim rushes to her room to change into jeans. Taylor is already dressed casually in jeans and a tee-shirt. They carefully take the bikes out of the garage. Taylor has her beloved Rosebud snuggled in the basket on the handlebars. Pedaling fast, they ride up and down the sidewalk. Neighborhood kids are admiring the shiny new bikes as a small group gathers.

A neighbor girl remarks, "I've never seen prettier bikes."

Taylor asks her, "Would you like to take a ride on my bike?" The little girl is thrilled and Taylor is happy to share. Taylor steadies the bike as the young girl climbs on. Kim decides she will not let anyone ride her bike.

The bike is a little too big for the neighbor girl to handle. She tries her best to control it. After one trip to the corner the bike begins to wobble and she crashes onto the gravel driveway. Rosebud lands in the dirt. Taylor rushes over to see if the girl is okay. Her knee is bleeding a little. Taylor picks some small pebbles off her knee and assures the girl, "You'll be alright."

Erika is disgusted, she has been watching from the window. She bolts out the front door screaming, "Taylor, as usual, you've made another bad decision. Pick up your stupid stuffed animal. It's filthy."

Taylor grabs Rosebud. With tears in her eyes, she gently brushes off her beloved teddy bear. Then she picks up her bike, "Oh good, there are no scratches on my bike." She walks back over to the neighbor girl, "Are you okay? You better go home and have your mom wash your knee."

Erika butts in, "You better worry about yourself, girl. I'm taking your bike away from you for one week."

Taylor's disappointed but knows it's better not to say much. She answers, "Yes, Mom." Taylor will not let this ruin her day. Twenty minutes later, she and Kim are playing dress-up in Kim's bedroom. Taylor opens a small trunk, "Isn't this stuff fun?" They drag out fancy dresses, high heel shoes, crazy looking hats, and piles of junk jewelry. Posing like fashion models is fun.

"Hold still Kim. Let me put make-up on you. I'll make you look beautiful." Very carefully she tries to do a neat job. They love playing dress-up. Taylor holds up a mirror for Kim so she can see herself in lipstick. "See how nice you look! Put on a necklace and a hat. Whoops." Taylor drops the mirror.

Kim hollers to her mother, "Taylor broke the handle off our new purple hand mirror from the Dollar Store!"

In a split second, Erika is standing in the doorway with her hands on her hips. Kim says, "Mommy she did it, I didn't."

Erika is pleased but sounds angry. Any time she has an opportunity to punish Taylor, it's a good day. She starts to vent, "Taylor, you make me sick! You're so reckless."

Taylor says, "I'm sorry, it was an accident."

Erika is furious, "You're impossible! Go down to the kitchen, you are going to sit on the barstool for one hour. Face the wall, you little monster. I just bought that mirror. What were you using it for?" Erika is vindictive enough to make a big deal over a cheap mirror just to punish Taylor.

"I was playing dress-up Mommy." Taylor begins to sob, "Can I go visit Gramma Diane?"

Erika commands, "Certainly not! You're not calling your grandmother! Hang up you little brat and give me that phone." Erika grabs it abruptly. All of Taylor's happiness is gone; she slumps on the stool.

It's very uncomfortable sitting on the stool with no back to lean on. Taylor will be relieved when the punishment is over. If only her father was home.

Off with the Door

The hour is up and Taylor asks for permission to get down and go to her room. She wants to go hug Rosebud. Starting upstairs, she doesn't know her stepmother has decided to follow behind. She goes into her room and quietly closes the door. Erika is out of control. There is a brief silence, then rage. She leaps up the stairs screaming, "You little brat, don't you slam that door in my face! Just wait! I'll be right back."

Erika is having an emotional breakdown and doesn't realize it as she impulsively vents her frustrations. She storms down the stairs to get a hammer and screwdriver. She's furious! Now back and breathing hard, she swings the hammer. *Bang! Bang!* She swings the hammer again. *Bang! Bang!* Erika screams, "I'm taking this door right off the hinges! You'll have no door to slam in my face."

Bracing herself against the wall, she lifts the door off. Taylor hugs Rosebud as she curls up in a fetal position on her bed. She whispers, "I'm scared Rosebud, I didn't slam the door. I wish daddy was home."

Taylor needs a drink of water. She starts to leave her room. Avoiding her stepmother, she moves with extreme caution. Taylor's afraid as she waits for Erika's next move. The uncertainty keeps her in her room. She'll go without a drink.

Taylor feels unsafe without a door on her bedroom. She stays in her room with Rosebud. Being near her stepmother feels dangerous. Suddenly she gets a glimpse of Erika's red dress as she hears quick footsteps storm toward her.

Her stepmother is back and Taylor begins to tremble. Erika says, "Your dad will be home tomorrow. I will tell him about all the trouble you have caused and you will be in bigger trouble." That evening she demands, "Taylor, help me get this door back on." Taylor climbs off her bed, Rosebud falls to the floor. Her lip is quivering as she helps her stepmother hold the door in place. Again, the sound of the hammer banging echoes through the upstairs bedrooms.

Kim shows up in the hall when she hears the commotion. Standing quietly, she watches them wrestle to put the door back on. Erika warns Kim, "You saw nothing, you know nothing. Do you understand?"

Kim drops her head, "Yes ma'am."

The next day Taylor relaxes, to her relief, daddy is home.

John announces, "It is so good to be back, how are all three of my girls?"

Taylor says, "We're fine, we're glad your home. I missed you, Daddy."

Everything appears calm and pleasant to John. Erika glares at Taylor, it's a warning and Taylor knows what the glare is for. Taylor decides not to tell her dad about her stepmother's violent outburst. She knows Erika will punish her with a greater vengeance if she does. Having her father home, she feels safe. John is relaxed and feels confident that his family is doing well.

Dinner is ready and John says grace. He compliments Erika on the delicious meal, "The stuffed green peppers are so good." John doesn't realize the peppers are right out of a frozen Stouffer's box. Erika is clever about covering the containers in the trash.

Erika says, "I've had some weird phone calls when you were gone. When I checked the phone, only your mother's number came up. There were six hang-up calls. I know your mother wouldn't do it. Do you think her phone could be out of order?" Erika is planting an idea in his head while she pretends to defend her mother-in-law.

John says, "If it's her phone number, she's the one who called."

Erika says, "Don't jump to conclusions, we really don't know who called and hung up."

Kim is ignored when she says, "I didn't hear the phone ring." Her voice is soft and no one noticed.

John is disgusted, "When does this craziness end? Calling my home and hanging up is not like my mom." He asks himself, is my mother losing it or is she just being mean? It's so childish. What is she trying to do? He is too exhausted to figure it out now.

Erika speaks up, "Relax John, it's no big deal."

"Let's go to bed early, Erika. We'll talk about this tomorrow. I'll read a story to Taylor and Kim tonight. The girls have already chosen the *Green Eggs and Ham* book by Dr. Seuss. I miss being with them. Can you join us for their prayers? The appointment I have tomorrow is complicated, I need a good night's rest." John and his daughters get cozy on the sofa as he begins to read. The girls snuggle up to him. He's thankful Erika minimized the phone problem.

The Hair Cut

John heads out to work the next morning. Erika is getting breakfast for the girls. After they finish their cheerios, Erika rushes them to the car. As she drives, an unexpected demand comes out of her mouth, another way to punish Taylor.

"Taylor, you are getting your hair cut short after school."

This confuses her, "Why Mommy? I don't want short hair. Is Kim getting her hair cut too?"

"No, Kim is keeping her long hair."

Taylor feels bad. She knows her dad loves her long golden hair. All day at school she worries about the haircut. She has a difficult time doing her schoolwork.

Ms. Reed asks, "Is there something wrong Taylor? It seems like your mind is miles away, you're not your happy self."

Taylor says, "Ms. Reed, tomorrow you won't see my long hair."

The teacher questions, "How do you feel about that?"

"I'm sad." Ms. Reed feels terrible for Taylor. She tells her that she is beautiful no matter how long or short her hair is.

Soon it's 3:30 and school's out. Erika is waiting in the long line of cars. Moms, dads, grandparents and nannies are patiently waiting for their little darlings to pop out the school door. Taylor and Kim spot their mom's Nissan. They toss their pink backpacks in the back before climbing aboard. Erika drives straight to Kid's Cuts.

Taylor begs her mom, "Please change your mind, I want to keep my long hair."

Erika doesn't listen. "You are not the boss! I'm tired of dealing with you."

Taylor is slow to get out of the car. Erika hollers at her, "Get a move on it, Taylor!" They enter Kid's Cuts. Taylor again begs her mom, "Please don't get my hair cut." Erika demands, "Now hush, I make the decisions!"

The hair designer, a short middle-aged woman with glasses, helps her get up into the chair. A blue cape is placed over her shoulders; the lady pulls out shiny silver scissors and a black comb. *Snip, snip! Chop, chop!* Pretty blonde curls fall to the floor. She hands Taylor a mirror and whirls the chair around. Taylor looks at the front and the back. Her bottom lip pouts out and a sad look comes over her face. She says, "I hate my haircut, daddy liked my long blond hair. I hate it!"

Erika snaps back, "Stop it, Taylor! Don't you dare tell your father you didn't want short hair."

All the way home, Taylor wipes her tears on her navy-blue T-shirt. She is careful not to cry out loud. Erika will scream at her if she makes a big fuss. Her heart is racing and she is devastated that her long hair is gone. There is a knot lodged in her throat.

They are almost home. Erika warns Taylor, "Walk in the house with a smile on your face. Do you hear me?" Kim trails behind too scared to speak.

"Yes ma'am," is her response.

"Let your dad know you like it."

John is shocked, "Wow, look at you, Taylor! You look cute, I didn't know you wanted short hair." He is disappointed but won't let it show.

Kim is glad she didn't have to get her hair cut. She feels sad for her sister but doesn't dare speak up. Erika speaks out, "She has been after me for weeks to get her hair cut, I finally gave in."

Taylor hears Erika's lie, she knows lies are wrong. That bothers her, but she doesn't dare to speak out. She asks her dad if she can go to her room. John says, "Sure Honey, can I have a hug first? Erika, she's growing up. You are wise to let her make some of her own decisions. I want her to be happy."

An hour later, John looks in her room. Taylor and Rosebud are snuggled under her pink blanket. He smiles as he sees his little girl sound asleep. He has no idea the pain his precious little girl is going through. John doesn't notice the big wet spot on her pillow caused by her flood of tears.

A House for Rosebud

Saturday morning comes, and Taylor's sadness has somewhat faded. She is anxious to create something special. John has given her a large empty box that contained equipment shipped to the office. He knew Taylor would create something out of it. She's excited to start.

Taylor has it all planned out in her mind. She works on it in the middle of the family room floor. It will be a house for Rosebud. Two hours later she asks Erika, "Can I paint green shutters on the windows?"

Erika says, "No, you'll have to use washable markers. No paint allowed."

Taylor finishes the shutters. She draws window boxes with flowers and a brown door. She is pleased with how it is turning out. All of a sudden Kim interferes, scribbling wildly in red marker over Taylor's house for her precious teddy bear. Taylor cries out, "Mommy look! Kim scribbled all over my house with a red magic marker, it's ruined!"

Erika is angry with Taylor. "Why can't you share it with your sister? You're a misfit! Whatever you do, wherever you go, there's trouble. I'm so sick of you."

Taylor, being an obedient child says, "I'm sorry, Mommy."

In a sharp voice, Erika tells her, "When your father gets home from his morning errands, he can take you to your grandmother's. Kim is going shopping with me, she wants a new outfit. I need a break from you. Your father has no idea what I have to put up with."

Taylor grabs Rosebud and goes to her room. She bellows out, "Yippee!" We're going to gramma Diane's, I love going there." No one heard except Rosebud.

Taylor stands by the window. She pulls back the white lace curtain so she can see when her dad's car pulls in the drive. As soon as John walks in, Erika asks him to call his mother and get her permission. Soon Taylor is all smiles. She knows her gramma will say yes.

John arrives at his parent's house. "Hi Mom, I guess you're expecting Taylor. She is so excited to come and spend time with you."

Diane is happy to have time with either grandchild. "I'm thrilled to have Taylor visit."

John tells her, "Erika will pick her up later in the day." He decides it is not a good time to confront his mother. It's supposed to be a happy day for Taylor. Diane is clue-less about what is happening behind the scenes; she has no idea that John is furious with her or that he believes she needs professional help.

Diane is surprised when she sees Taylor's hair. "You got your hair cut. You look cute in short hair, Honey."

In truth, Diane is disappointed that Taylor's long hair was gone. Taylor says, "Are you sure you like it? Gramma, will you keep a secret? I begged mommy not to get my hair cut, she wouldn't listen. I hate my hair cut!"

Diane is disturbed by this. "Taylor, let's make cookies and have a tea party. We won't let it ruin our time together."

Diane gets the little oak table and chairs out. All of a sudden Taylor sees another teddy bear seated next to Rosebud. "Gramma, where did this brown bear come from? Rosebud has a friend."

Diane tells her, "That is Ollie, your father's little friend when he was young like you."

Taylor says, "That is so cool, I love coming to visit you, Gramma."

Soon the smell of cookies fills the room. Diane places them on a small blue-and-white plate. Diane asks her to offer thanks. Taylor begins, "Thank you, Jesus, for cookies and gramma, Amen."

Diane allows her to pour the tea. "Gramma, tell me again about the little dishes."

"They are blue willow, made in Japan. I had tea parties with them when I was young."

Taylor realizes the blue and white dishes are very special. "We have to be very careful when we wash them." Diane is enjoying the tea party as much as Taylor. She is a wonderful loving grandmother.

Suddenly, they hear a car come to a screech as it pulls in the drive. Taylor wishes she could stay longer. Erika bursts in the door saying, "I'm back early. Taylor, clean up this mess. I'm in a hurry."

Taylor says, "It's not a mess, it's a tea party."

Erika retorts with a sharp voice, "Don't sass me!"

Just then Edward arrives home. "This is good timing, I get to see some of my favorite people."

Erika answers, "You are looking great, Edward."

He replies, "Thanks, Erika. Where's Kim?"

"She fell asleep in the car. Thanks for putting up with Taylor."

Diane is holding back tears thinking that her beautiful little granddaughter is being mistreated.

Taylor clutches her teddy bear as Erika rushes her to the car. Diane felt Erika's remark, "putting up with Taylor," was very telling. She doesn't bring it up to Edward. She realizes he wouldn't read anything into it. Erika can do no wrong in his eyes.

Soon they're back home and John is anxious to hear about her visit, "How was your day with gramma?"

"Oh Daddy, it was so much fun. We made cookies for our tea party. Rosebud has a new friend, your old teddy bear Ollie. He was sitting at the little table, he looks old, but he is still cute."

John says, "My goodness, does gramma still have Ollie?" John turns to Kim and asks, "How was your day sweetie?"

"I went shopping with mommy and she bought me a beautiful pink shirt. I'll go get it, Daddy, so you can see how special it is."

As Kim models, John tells her, "Your shirt is very pretty. Did you and your mom see any in your sister's size?"

Kim answers, "I guess we couldn't find one for Taylor." John doesn't realize that Erika didn't even look for one.

The girls go in to watch cartoons. John asks, "Erika, how did my mother treat you when you stopped to pick up Taylor?"

She takes a deep breath, "I asked her if the church cookbook was back from the printers. She said, 'What cookbook? I don't know what you're talking about.' John, she was the head of the project. That is concerning."

John admits, "Mom just isn't the same, this continues to be very hard for me." Erika doesn't miss a chance to discredit Diane and plant doubts in his mind about his mother.

The next morning, Erika calls Nancy and tells her how she made Taylor cry. She explains how she insisted Taylor get her hair cut short. Nancy reminds Erika again, "Why did you do that? It's about your mother-in-law, not John's daughter."

Erika explains, "I can't help myself with Taylor. She irritates me, just looking at her makes me angry. I was never that beautiful when I was young."

"Do you think Taylor will tell her father that you're mean to her?"

Erika tells her, "No, I put the fear of God in her and make her think it's her fault."

All of a sudden, Erika remembers Kim is going home with a friend after school. "I'll talk to you later, Nancy. I need some time before I pick up Taylor. Kim will be home later."

After they hang up, Erika puts a DVD on to watch a movie. Getting deeply engrossed in the story, she is late to pick up Taylor. She isn't worried about it. When she finally gets to the school, she is met by Ms. Reed. The teacher firmly lets Erika know, "I missed an important appointment I had after school. I better have a meeting with Taylor's father."

Erika sets her straight, "I'm their mother, thank you. You will call me! Come on Taylor, we are leaving." The door slams, Taylor is scared and remains silent on the way home. She feels bad for the way her stepmother spoke to Ms. Reed. Taylor loves her teacher.

Dinner Disaster

One hour later, Kim is dropped off by her friend's mother. Taylor wants Kim to tell her about the visit and the fun they had. Abruptly, Erika interrupts to announce, "Your father is working late, so I'm not cooking tonight. Get the peanut butter and grape jelly out. Taylor, I want you to help Kim make her sandwich."

"Yes Mommy."

She lays out the bread and makes two sandwiches. Carefully, she gets two glasses out for milk. Opening the refrigerator, Taylor grabs the full gallon of milk. It is so heavy, it slips out of her hands and the cap pops off. It splashes on the sandwiches and falls on the floor. There's milk everywhere, Taylor is scared now. She's on her hands and knees with a towel trying to clean up the mess. Her jeans and white T-shirt are wet with milk. She wrings the towel out in the sink, and then grabs two big dry ones to finish the job.

Kim tattles, "Mommy, Taylor spilled the milk."

Tears are rolling down Taylor's cheeks as she mops up the milk as fast as she can. She is scared. She knows her mother is going to be in a rage. Erika enters the room with her hands on her hips. She screams, "I can't believe this! I am so fed up with you! Are you clumsy or stupid? Clean this mess up while Kim and I go to McDonald's to eat."

Taylor says, "I'm sorry Mommy, it was too heavy for me." Her eyes are wet with tears.

Kim feels bad now, "Mommy, can Taylor go with us?"

Erika blurts out with a loud voice, "No, she has a soggy sandwich to eat and a floor to mop up. Let's go."

Taylor is hurting but is convinced it was her own fault. She throws the wet sandwiches in the garbage. She wishes she could have gone to McDonald's too. She has never been left home alone nor has she ever felt so frightened. After making another peanut butter and jelly sandwich, she sits down to eat. She wants to call her gramma, but knows that her stepmother would punish her. She wishes Erika was not her stepmother.

Her stepmother and sister get home just as she finishes. Erika says, "You could have done a better job on this floor. Get another towel and go over the floor again. This time use soap and water. Get a move on it, Taylor! You made this mess!"

John's daughters are both in bed when he gets home. The floor is sticky. He doesn't ask questions, but instead, he gets out the mop. Erika doesn't let on how ugly the evening was. She says, "One of the girls spilled a little milk, it was no big deal. They are really great girls! Accidents happen." Erika in her sweet voice says, "Let's go in the family room and watch the evening news and relax. How was your day, Honey?"

He answers, "I had a very productive day."

She tells him, "I love Taylor and Kim. They're such a pleasure." John is so relieved to hear this. He believes that Erika adores the girls and controls her anger when she is with them. Life would be better if only his mother wasn't creating a problem. He often has stress at the office and he wishes his private life was easier. All he wants is a happy, peaceful life with his daughters and beautiful wife.

Early the next morning John informs Erika, "Dad and Mom are going to New York for a few days. Dad's due at Mt. Cedar Hospital for tests on his pacemaker. Erika, would you please help me out by picking up their mail?"

Erika says, "Of course, no problem. Does his pacemaker need to be replaced? I hope he'll be okay, I'll pray for him. You know how much I love your father."

As he is about to leave for Tampa, he hugs her goodbye, "Hey, is that purple bathrobe new? You look amazing in it!"

She admits, "It's new, but it was on sale."

"Honey, whatever you paid it was worth it. You look fabulous!"

She asks, "How long will you be out of town? Is Mark going?" He answers, "Yes, and yes."

"Mark and I hope we'll get this case finished in two or three days. I'll call you." What Erika doesn't know is that John has located an "Elizabeth Keppel" in Baton Rouge. He is going to visit her as soon as his schedule permits. He is hoping to find a way to help Erika get rid of unresolved anger, perhaps by reconnecting her with her mother.

Erika is in no hurry. She waits two days before going to the Barringer's house. The mailbox is full. She's surprised to see two painters there; the men are having coffee and doughnuts in their red pickup truck. Erika with a smile says, "Good morning guys, the Barringer's know that you're here?"

Tony tells her, "We've done work for them for years. They left instructions for us to paint. We are about to go to the Benjamin Moore store to pick up paint for the garage doors."

Erika volunteers to go for them while they prepare the surface. At the paint store, Erika switches the color. What was dove gray is now a toasted beige. She returns and hands Tony a gallon can of the new color. The men begin to paint.

Tony notices the color is different than he usually uses for the trim on the Barringer's house. Erika assures him the color is right. The men proceed to paint. Tony remarks, "Don't get paint on that pretty white jacket ma'am." She thanks him. Erika will use this opportunity for her benefit. She has full access to the Barringer's home.

Erika remembers why she's there as she puts the mail on the table. She then goes upstairs to the master bedroom. Diane's study Bible is on the bed. Gathering up the powder blue sheet, Bible and all, she stuffs it all in the bathroom hamper. Back downstairs, as she is leaving, she notices Erwin Lutzer's book on the hall table. Walking into the beautiful white kitchen, she ponders what to do next. Erika decides to put the book in the oven and leave.

Back in her Nissan, she calls Nancy to tell her what she did. Nancy is puzzled, "Explain."

Is Diane Losing Her Mind?

Erika begins, "Diane will believe she's losing it. I changed the paint color the painters are using. I put her Bible in the hamper and her book in the oven. She'll blame herself, trust me. This will drive her crazy, I love it!"

Nancy admits, "Very clever, your ideas don't surprise me at all." Erika ends the call and drives home. The Barringers are due back home later today. They enter the gate at Whitney Chase and pull into their drive. Edward removes the luggage. Diane takes a quick glance at the garage doors and is shocked and disappointed. "It's beige! It's supposed to be gray."

"Edward, call Tony. The garage doors look terrible! They no longer match the trim on our house." Diane is very disappointed and upset.

Edward quickly responds, "Calm down dear, it's only paint. We will have it repainted."

Diane says, "I must have selected the wrong number in the computer."

Tony says, "Your daughter-in-law picked up the paint for us and assured us that it was the right color."

Edward speaks up, "All I know is, it wasn't Erika's fault. There must be a simple explanation."

After a quick trip to get the correct color, the garage doors are soon repainted. All is forgotten, but Diane is dismayed. How could she have gotten the paint wrong? She has used the same gray for five years. She is convinced she must have confused the paint numbers. All evening Diane is concerned, how did she get the color wrong?

The Cherry on Top

Today is another school day. After the girls are dropped off, Erika goes shopping. The mall is unusually quiet in the mornings. The rush hasn't started yet. Erika enters her favorite clothing store. Browsing through the latest styles, she notices the military look. This isn't what would normally appeal to her, but it intrigues her today. It's sporty and has a sense of power. Selecting a few items in her size, she goes to the dressing room. The outfits fit perfectly. She pulls the olive drab jersey over her head and tucks it in her pants. She finishes the look with a long-sleeve camouflage jacket. Standing tall, she feels strong and powerful. She will control her own destiny.

The purchase is made, and Erika returns home wearing her new outfit. The thought comes to her, she needs boots. She starts poking around in her closet. "Where did I put those damn boots?" Under three shoes, a hanger, and a lid to a shoe box, she finds her brown boots. The struggle to put them on is worth it because they handsomely complete her outfit.

Erika feels confident about her new look. She wants to tell Nancy, so she pushes redial. The voice on the other line says, "I've been waiting two days for your call." Erika wants to tell her about the new purchase, but Nancy has something different on her mind.

"Wait until you hear this! I just discovered an app that allows you to make your mother-in-law's car windows go up and down at your will. Do it when she's driving, it will make her crazy." Nancy explains the process explicitly and Erika is listening intently.

"Thanks, this is the cherry on top!"

"You know the door combination to your mother-in-law's BMW, right?"

Erika answers, "Yes, but please go over the three steps again so I can follow your directions to set it up. You're a genius Nancy. Let's talk later, I have work to do. This is going to be great! I have the combination for her car door. I'll wait until it's parked at the hospital on a day she volunteers."

The app is set. Erika remembers the special meeting at church that Diane will be attending which starts at 6:00. As her mother-in-law is traveling west on Jackson Road, all of the car windows go down. One mile later, they go back up. This repeats once more before she pulls into the parking lot. Immediately she calls her husband to tell him what happened.

"Edward, it was the weirdest thing, I never touched the buttons. My car windows went up and down by themselves."

"Honey, are you sure you didn't push the buttons? How could that be? We'll discuss this tonight."

As soon as he's off the phone he calls his son. "Your mom's memory seems to be fading. We must get her some help. Remember when I found her Bible in the clothes hamper and now she believes her car windows went down and back up without touching the buttons. This is worrisome, John. Will you find a good doctor for your mother?"

"I will, Dad. Pray she can overcome this. Mom is too young to be losing her memory. We need her to be healthy. I'll find a doctor this afternoon and get back to you soon."

Unfortunately, no appointments are immediately available, so John makes one for a week later. Unexpectedly, Diane's father dies of a massive stroke. With travel and the funeral, that appointment for Diane had to be canceled.

Weeks later, Erika hears John discussing his grandfather's will with his mother on the phone. The following morning John's up early. He has to drive to Winston-Salem for a bank meeting. As Erika hears him up, she stumbles out of bed. The sun is just rising. Putting on her white terry cloth robe, she grabs her hairbrush and runs it through her shoulder-length hair. Hearing the shower, she decides it's safe to take a peek into her husband's briefcase. Diane's father's funeral was three weeks ago, and John has a copy of the will.

He hasn't shown her or discussed it with her. She's been curious and now is her chance to read it. Being sneaky doesn't bother her. She is surprised by its contents and reads on.

Dr. Harrison left his only child, Diane Victoria, the entire estate worth just over four million dollars.

Upon her death, it goes to John, his only grandchild. Evil thoughts cross Erika's mind. Suddenly she hears the water in the shower stop. Quickly the papers are put back in his briefcase.

She goes downstairs and plugs in the coffee; cinnamon rolls go in the oven. She carefully slices the hot rolls so the butter will melt into them. Erika sprinkles a little extra cinnamon sugar mix on top. John's in a cheerful mood when he enters the kitchen; he's pleasantly surprised to see his wife has made such an effort. The aroma of coffee and cinnamon smells delicious. It brings a smile to his face; she gets a huge hug for the effort. They enjoy a quick breakfast.

Erika comments, "How handsome you look in that powder blue shirt. It looks so sharp! Your tie has the same shade of blue in the stripe. Just maybe I'm getting you more conscientious about your clothes. I'm good for you. I just have a feeling you're going to have a successful day."

"Thanks, Erika, your support is important to me. Would you have time to run an errand for me today?"

The Oil Change

"Always there to help," she reassures him.

"I promised to take my mother's car for an oil change, it's overdue. I told her I'd do it but I'm just too busy. Would you please call the BMW garage and have them schedule it? Do you mind?"

She answers, "Don't be silly, I'm happy to help out."

After a quick kiss, he thanks her and heads for the office.

After she drops Taylor and Kim off at school, she dials Nancy's number. Explaining what she read in Dr. Harrison's will, she pauses to get Nancy's reaction. Before she has time to answer, Erika mentions, "I've promised to get my mother-in-law's oil changed at the BMW Service Center."

Nancy's ears perk up.

"Get the brake fluid drained out at the same time. You can't get that done at a BMW garage. What a great opportunity!"

Erika realizes that could cause an accident. She processes Nancy's comment, "There is a mechanic that I can bribe into doing it for me. I need to look into this. I'll get back to you."

Before they hang up, Nancy warns, "Be careful!"

Next, she calls Ralph and explains the situation. Ralph's towing service had come to her rescue when she was once speeding and ended up in a ditch. She saw him again when his mistress ended up in ICU following a ruptured appendix. He was there every day to see her. The patient told Erika that Ralph was married with three children and that they had been having an affair for several months. His wife didn't have a clue. Erika stored the information in her mean mind.

Erika rushes to get all the arrangements organized. Then she phones her mother-in-law to let her know she's on the way to pick up her car for the oil change. Diane has heard of her fast driving and is concerned with her driving the BMW.

Within the hour, Erika pulls into Ralph's garage. He knows she has a secret she can hold over him.

She steps out of the car, being careful not to step in an oily puddle on the floor. Ralph's clothes are covered with oil and the smell is hard to ignore. Erika asks, "If you drain the brake fluid out, how far can it be driven?"

He answers, "It can be driven thirty miles before the brakes go out."

"Go for it Ralph, let's get it done." She enters his office and looks for a seat. Next to the weathered roll-top desk, covered with unorganized papers, she makes herself comfortable. An ashtray on a stand nearby is full of cigarette butts, the stink is awful. She ignores the smell and grabs a Hollywood magazine to read the gossip. Two hours later, and well worth the wait, the job is finished. She pays in cash before thanking him.

Ralph doesn't trust her, "Are we even now?" Erika devilishly smiles and chuckles.

She feels no guilt when she returns the BMW to her mother-in-law. Diane thanks her daughter-in-law and repays her with a check.

Diane will soon be on her way to the Kannapolis Post Office to renew her passport. She looks much younger than her age of 62. Today she looks even more stunning in her white pantsuit. Her rose-colored blouse reflects on her face. On her lapel is an antique broach with semi-precious stones in rose tones. It's a family heirloom that once belonged to Edward's grandmother. She always dresses with class and style.

Waving goodbye to Erika, she backs out of her drive and heads for Kannapolis. Twenty-eight miles later, she comes to a warning sign, "Reduce Speed / Construction Ahead". Her brakes aren't working as she tries to slow down. She downshifts, the car slows some. Frightened, she screams, "Lord Jesus, help me!" The BMW crashes into the barricades, boards splinter and fly into the air. As the car jolts to a stop, Diane is thrust forward. The airbags deploy. She's fortunate that she only sustained a few bruises and thankful to be alive after the frighten-ing experience. For several minutes her heart refuses to stop pounding.

A workman helps her out of the car. "Lady, God was with you, the bridge is out. Another six feet and you would have gone into the river. The water is raging after yesterday's storm. The barricades stopped your car; or was it your guardian angel?"

Diane tells them, "My brakes failed."

Still shaken and her heart pounding, she calls Grace to come and take her home. Diane doesn't want to put stress on her husband. Edward gets a call, "I was in a minor accident today, it wasn't my fault. Don't be concerned, I'm fine. My car is being towed for repair. Grace is coming to pick me up."

Edward tells her that he will leave the office and come straight to the site of the accident. He is concerned about his wife and tells her, "Diane, I am so thankful you are okay." She reiterates that she is fine and that Grace is on her way. He tells her "Go home and rest; don't worry about the car. Call me if you need anything, I love you."

"I'll be fine, not to worry."

Grace arrives thirty minutes later, she is glad to be available for her friend. She assures Diane that she will take her to the BMW garage when her car is repaired. On the drive back to Whitney Chase, the two friends remind each other how good God is. Diane thanks her for the ride.

"Grace, God sent his guardian angels to protect me."

Diane has calmed down and feels better. She has no clue that brake fluid had been drained from her car.

Three days later, Grace takes her to pick up the car. Her BMW is repaired and is just like new. The man at the garage informed Diane that the brake fluid was checked and filled. There was no leak. "I've seen brake fluid low, but never empty. It's a mystery how it all got drained out. That doesn't happen." Diane reflects on God's grace and knows it is sufficient for her.

The Car Search

Two weeks later John is concerned about the condition of Erika's older Nissan. Complaints of it stalling out causes concern for the safety of his family. He has asked his mother to take Erika shopping for a new SUV. No matter how inconvenient, Diane is always willing to help out her son. John's schedule at the courthouse is demanding, making it impossible for him to take her himself. Erika has convinced him that she might get hives when she's with his mother. John overlooks that for now. Finding a safe vehicle is far more important.

Diane's on her way to pick up her daughter-in-law. They head out to visit various auto showrooms. Diane begins to share the scary experience she had a couple of weeks ago, "I was on my way to Kannapolis when my brakes failed. I crashed into a large barricade. It was frightening, I came close to going into the river. What a horrible ordeal, I was frozen with fear! God sent his guardian angels to protect me."

Diane has no idea that Erika was behind her car windows malfunctioning or that her viper of a daughter-in-law had plotted to kill her. Erika feigns sympathy saying, "How frightening. I feel bad for what you went through."

Diane answers, "You have no idea! I was terrified and could have been killed. I'm ok now. It's a new day, let's get started. We need to find you a new SUV, I'm very happy to help."

They start the search. It has been a long exhausting day visiting five different dealerships. They have seen Hondas, Buicks, Jeeps, and Chevys. Erika decides she wants the first car she saw that morning. They head back to the Subaru dealership. Diane excuses herself to use the restroom.

When she returns to the showroom the salesman tells her, "Your daughter-in-law is out on the lot taking a second look at the Subaru Ascent."

Diane walks over to the one Erika likes; she is nowhere to be found. She calls her name, "Erika, Erika." Diane is puzzled. She calls again, "Erika, Erika." There's no response. Turning to go back in the showroom, she sees Erika's head pop up. Diane confronts her. Erika claims she was checking out the radio. Confused and frustrated, Diane lets her know she isn't buying her story.

Diane tells her, "I've spent all day trying to help you and now you're hiding from me? If you want that SUV, go to the desk and do the paperwork." Diane feels like she is dealing with an insolent child. Erika is amused by seeing her mother-in-law wrangled.

The trip home was tense, Diane finally breaks the silence.

"They will go over your new Subaru. I'll bring you back tomorrow and you can drive it home." Diane gives her a loving smile as she gets out of her car, to assure her that she is not upset anymore. Erika thanks her for all of her help. She loves playing with Diane's mind and keeping her off balance.

As soon as Erika gets home, she calls John at the office.

She blares out, "I bought a Subaru!"

He says, "I hope it is a Forester."

"Nope, it's the new Subaru Ascent. It has a turbo engine and is safer for the girls. You'll love the color, it's a pale silver with gray leather interior. It has all the safety features." What she doesn't say is that it is 17K more than the Forester.

"You will not believe what your mother accused me of. She said I was hiding from her at the car dealership. She is crazy. She was talking to me like I was a child. Did she think she was with Taylor or Kim?"

John is unraveled now and this adds to his concern. "I am very worried about her."

Erika tells him, "Your mother told me I need counseling. Can you believe that? I am very upset with her, but I'll get over it, I always do. Stay out of it John. I'm a big girl, I can take care of myself. I won't ride with her tomorrow; Heidi will take me to pick up the Ascent."

John says, "I'm sorry Erika. I'm trying to find mother the best doctor in the area. Next, you and I are going house hunting. I want you to pick out the home you want. Our home has all the memories of Amy, we need a fresh start. You deserve to be happy for all that my mother has put you through. I've spoken with a realtor. We will soon start to look for a new home."

Erika Gets Her Mansion

Erika sees all her dreams coming true, a new car, and now a new home. Best of all, she has John catering to her every whim. Unexpectedly, John has an opening in his schedule. He's anxious to go house hunting with his wife. A beautiful woman deserves a beautiful home.

The real estate agent has a list of must-haves at John's request. She has three homes lined up for them to see, each home has six bedrooms and six and one-half baths. Erika is overwhelmed and excited. After several hours, they decide on the house in a gated community. It is a spectacular two-story country French Manor with slate blue shutters and a circular drive. It has a beautiful swimming pool with a fountain. The outside kitchen is great for entertaining and there's a television over the stone fireplace in the outside sitting area. Inside, the large kitchen is open to the family room and the master bath is extraordinary with white marble floors. The couple will each have separate, generous sized closets, hers with a crystal chandelier. She is awestruck!

Erika says, "This is the perfect house, the girls will each have their own bedroom and bath."

John is amazed, "You're always thinking of what's best for my daughters." They both agree that this is the perfect home for their family. Papers are signed.

John's phone rings, Mark is on the line. "I hate to bother you, but this is an emergency." John realizes the importance, "Erika, grab your yellow raincoat from the car, it's getting chilly. It looks like I have to leave." Mark breaks in again, "We need you at the office right away." Erika understands as he rushes off.

The agent reassures Erika that she will take her to pick up the girls at school. After the big commission she just made, she feels she must help out. Twenty minutes later, Taylor and Kim are in the car. On the way home, Erika tells the girls to decide on a color for their new bedrooms.

"Your father bought us a big new house. It's awesome! It's a mansion!" Soon they're home enjoying their after-school snack. Afterwards, Taylor and Kim go to the front room to play. Erika can hardly wait to call her friend. Nancy takes the call. Erika is all excited and yells out, "Wish you could see this house John is buying me, it is fabulous!" She tells Nancy all the details. Her friend is very impressed. Erika then tells her what she did to Diane during the car search, "I hid on the floor of the SUV. Yes, you heard right."

Nancy says, "What in the world did you do that for?"

Erika answers, "I loved it. It was hilarious! She called my name several times, but I didn't answer. Then when I thought she had left, I poked my head up and she saw me. I wanted to burst out laughing but couldn't. I told

John. Of course, I twisted the story and made her look insane. He believes his mother needs help. It's working! I'm driving her crazy!"

Nancy is amazed at Erika's cleverness, "I would believe you are really evil but that can't be. To be evil there would have to be a Satan and we know that is a fable. Truth is, if there was a Satan, there would have to be a God. No one with a brain could believe that."

Erika thinks about it, "Why be concerned with Satan if he doesn't exist?" Erika agrees with Nancy, there is nothing after death. "Those so-called Christians are pitiful for what they believe."

Nancy shares, "You're born, you die, and you're worm food." Erika comes back with "We think alike. Talk to you later, bye for now."

Just then, Taylor and Kim come running into the kitchen. Kim asks, "Mommy, can we draw pictures to hang on the refrigerator?"

They get her permission, anything to keep them busy and out of her hair. Soon Kim calls her mom to see her art, Erika raves about Kim's picture. Immediately, it goes up on the refrigerator. Taylor, who is truly talented, shows her mom her drawing. Erika doesn't compliment Taylor or hang it on the refrigerator. It's tossed on the kitchen counter as if it has no significance, a heartless act.

Taylor notices, "You don't like mine, I'll put it in a secret place until daddy gets home."

When John walks in, the first picture he sees is Kim's.

"Good job Kim. I like the flowers you drew. That's a good-looking vase too."

Taylor runs in with her art and John loves it. He asks, "May I hang both pictures in my law office?" They feel proud; their faces light up with big smiles. He reminds them, "Remember the brown and white puppies you drew? They are still on display in the conference room."

John's happy to be home with his family. Erika is on her best behavior.

Taylor tells Kim, "I think I smell pizza."

"Your mom has a surprise; she has baked your favorite pizza, triple cheese and pepperoni." She serves the pizza and pours milk for the girls. John gets two cold Pepsi's out for Erika and himself. After pizza, Erika instructs the girls, "Run upstairs and put on your blue pajamas, then you can play a game with your father." It's a happy evening, John feels good about his family. He still has no idea how horrible his wife can be.

It's a pleasant time at home, Erika is thinking about their new fabulous house. Taylor gets the Candy Land game out. It's an older board game that Gramma Diane gave the girls. John plays the game with his daughters and they're all smiles. Playing games with their dad is always lots of fun. Taylor wins the first game, Kim wins the second time. John enjoys the evening. He loves to see his daughters happy. Erika notices they have finished the games. "Okay girls, go brush your teeth, it's bedtime. Your father and I will be up to say prayers with you." With a pleasant smile on his face, John remarks, "Erika, you're such a good fit in my life. I truly appreciate you."

Heidi's Visit

Early the next day Erika is surprised when Heidi stops by. She welcomes her in. They share small talk and coffee. The girls come running in when they hear Heidi's voice. Heidi gives each of them a big hug. She can't help but notice Kim's darling blue and white outfit. She asks them how school is going. Soon they are off to get their coloring books and crayons out. Heidi then confronts Erika, "Every time I see the girls, Kim is dressed in adorable outfits, Taylor is always dressed in drab blue jeans and plain shirts. What's up with that?"

Her remark makes Erika furious. "Are you trying to say that I favor one daughter over the other? I don't appreciate it and it's none of your business! Don't the girls seem happy to you?"

Heidi stays calm and says, "I'm your friend, Erika. Do you think you may be treating Taylor like your mother treated you?" Erika becomes silent. Then she confides in Heidi, "I find myself being rough on Taylor. I treat her unfairly. It's like I can't help it, anger takes control of me. Please keep this to yourself."

Heidi has to be at work in twenty minutes, so she can't stay long. She feels very bad after hearing Erika admit that she treats Taylor unfairly. She is very concerned; she can't overlook this emotional abuse.

As she leaves she tells Erika, "I will pray for you."

John is in Chicago on business; that evening he calls home, "How are my girls?"

Erika has a good report ready, "Taylor and Kim are in bed fast asleep. We had a Bible story, night snack, teeth brushed, and prayers said."

John replies, "You are wonderful Erika, I love you. I don't know how I got along without you. I wish I was home with you and the girls tonight."

Erika says, "The bad news is your mother has accused me of taking her lamp receipt. She wants to return it to the store, but they won't accept it without proof of purchase. I don't blame her John. I'd be upset myself. She paid $395.00 for the lamp. Maybe she misplaced it and forgot. It is a shame, that's a lot of money. John, you know I wouldn't take her receipt."

"Erika, I certainly know you'd never take it...absolutely." He has no idea Erika crumpled it up and threw it away. John buys into the lie and becomes even more upset with his mother.

"This is it Erika, I'm putting an end to this!" He refuses to listen to his wife's pleas not to confront his mother. He hangs up the phone. Erika has protected his mother every time. They have kept some things from his dad because of his heart. He decides to fly home a day early from Chicago. Disgusted, he drives straight to his mother's house. John appreciates Erika for being so patient with his mother. This has gone on long enough; he will protect his wife at any cost. It's time for action. Diane has overstepped and has now lost her son.

The Tirade

It's a beautiful late afternoon. Diane is in a cheerful mood, relaxing on the screened-in porch with Lucy their sheepdog. The phone rings, it's her son. John blares out, "I'm on my way to your house and I'm furious. Mother, you will answer for everything you've done when you stand before God." Diane is speechless. Why is he so mad?

Diane's caught unaware and is confused. She has never known him to be so upset. What did she do? Why is John so angry with her? Diane agonizes over the way he is yelling at her. All of a sudden, she hears the dial tone. He has hung up on his mother.

John is breathing heavy as he enters the house. His voice is loud, "Mother, why are you trying to destroy my marriage? You told Erika she needs counseling, but it's you that needs professional help. You told me that Erika actually hid in a car from you. Am I going to have to move my family far away from you to protect them? Erika and I just signed for a new home in the area, but I'm canceling the purchase today. I'm looking for a job in another state. And another thing, I'm sure you forgot where you put your lamp receipt. Why would you accuse my wife?" John doesn't give his mother the opportunity to explain.

He then tells her that he's been trying to find her psychiatric help for her problem. "Mother, you haven't seen my wife cry and tremble because of what you've said and done to her."

John abruptly leaves and slams the door when he walks out. Diane is devastated. How can she tell Edward? She wonders what she did to turn John against her? She'd never seen him so angry. She never accused Erika of taking the receipt. Why did John assume that? Confused and broken-hearted, she goes to bed early, tossing and turning, never sleeping a wink. How is she going to tell Edward? He will be devastated. What about his heart problem? He'll soon be home from Rotary, but she will wait until tomorrow to tell him.

Now it's seven o'clock in the morning, she hears Edward in the kitchen pouring a cup of coffee. Diane is exhausted; the smell of coffee doesn't tempt her. She tells her husband, "I have some bad news. You better sit down."

Edward responds, "I lost a case yesterday, I don't need any more bad news."

Diane tells him, "This is worse, brace yourself."

He says, "Hit me with it, I can take it."

"John is looking for a job out of state. It is all my fault Edward, I'm so sorry."

He says, "That can't be true, they just bought a house."

Diane feels she must have unknowingly upset Erika in some way. Edward is at a loss for words. John is their only child and Taylor and Kim are their only grandchildren. He can't bear to lose them. He is crushed in spirit. Diane loves her husband and is concerned about his health. She pulls herself together and prays for strength. Edward hugs his wife before leaving for the office. As he walks out the door, he says, "God will see us through this."

Diane lies down on the sofa, she is wiped out. Four hours later she's surprised when she checks the time. Being so tired, she managed to fall asleep for a few hours.

She has promised she would bake blueberry muffins for Taylor and Kim. She may not get another chance. Overwhelmed with sadness, she goes to the kitchen to get started.

Opening the pantry, she grabs her blue and white striped apron. Diane, with tears in her eyes, mixes up the blueberry batter. The oven is heating up. She pours the batter into a muffin pan lined with individual papers. Soon there are ten muffins ready to pop in the oven. Minutes later she smells smoke! The phone rings, Heidi's on the line with a question about church. Diane is frustrated, "I can't talk now, my kitchen is full of smoke. The smoke detector is blasting off."

Heidi calms her down, "Diane, turn off the oven and open the window."

The smoke begins to clear as Diane tells Heidi, "My guardian angel must have urged you to call. Thanks Heidi, you were a big help."

After they hang up, Diane sees her Erwin Lutzer book half burned up in the oven. She is now really concerned about her mental health. She cleans up the kitchen then sits down to rest. Why did she put the book in the oven? Why is she forgetting things? Feeling despondent, she leans back and rests her head on the back of the wing back chair.

Just then the phone rings again. It's Grace, her faithful friend. "Diane, I felt like I should call you. Lately you've seemed concerned and upset."

Diane tells her, "I'm depressed. I'm going through a hard time. I'm forgetting things. There are so many things I can't remember. John and his family are moving out of state. It doesn't get much worse than that."

Grace asks her, "Why are they moving?"

Diane admits, "It's all my fault, I guess I've done something that upset Erika. My memory isn't what it used to be, so I really can't remember what I did. Once Edward found my Bible in the hamper wrapped in a sheet. He's worried about me. John said I will answer to God for everything I've done."

Grace Figures It Out

Grace interrupts, "Stop it Diane! Just stop it! Wait a minute, it doesn't make sense." Grace ponders the problem, suddenly the light comes on. "I have known you for many years. We've been close; you have always had a sharp mind. I am starting to wonder about Erika, let's take an inventory of events. Your study Bible has two hundred pages. It's very heavy, just like mine. You'd know if it were in a sheet. Oh, and maybe you were given the wrong day to meet at the bridal shop. Erika spilled cream on your skirt and she gave you a used gift. I believe she damaged the handle on the freezer. I believe she changed the paint color. She hid in the car and might have put your book in the oven. She changed your recipe. Should I go on? Did Erika take your car for inspection? Maybe it wasn't taken to the BMW garage. Could she have had someone else do the work on your car and drain the brake fluid? I think she is trying to destroy you or even kill you. At the least, she is trying to make you look like you are losing your mind. You didn't want John to marry her, she is getting even."

Diane ponders it, Grace may be right. She has seen it but couldn't face the real truth about Erika. It was easier for her to blame herself. John and Edward would never believe that Erika could be so devious.

Grace asks, "Do you really believe she told you about their Christmas in Hilton Head? What about the lamp receipt or Taylor's haircut? How did your car windows go up and down?"

"Thank you for pointing these things out, Grace. Will you pray with me? I need wisdom and the grace to forgive Erika and see how to help her."

Grace says, "Let's pray."

Back at the law office, Edward has his office door closed. He is on his knees praying that John and his family will not move out of state.

Meanwhile, John is wrapping up his last case at the office. He wants all the work for his father's law firm completed. He calls Erika to tell her, "I will be home late. I'm wrapping up my final work here. I already have an interview in Denver, and it sounds very promising. I canceled the purchase of the new house."

On the phone, Erika is seething. She never thought it would come to this. She leaves a desperate message for her evil friend. "Nancy, I'm in a bad spot. I am not going to give up that fabulous house John and I signed for. I have always pictured myself in a house like that. There's no way I'm moving to Colorado." Erika has lost control, and control is everything to her. "I need your advice, Nancy. Help me." Erika quickly hangs up.

Erika confronts John when he gets home. He is adamant about moving. His determination to move without Erika's consent makes her very angry. She thinks that he is over-reacting. She tries to hit his soft spot, "What about the girls' school and their friends?" She continues, "What about our new home, my job, our church. You're not considering all that our lives entail here." She takes a deep breath, "John, we can stay away from your mother and put her out of our lives." When he doesn't seem to care about what she is saying, she goes into a rage! "We are not moving! You are a jerk for not considering my feelings!" She picks up a bowl on the table and throws it at him. It barely misses his head and crashes into the kitchen cabinet, shattering all over the floor. The bowl was a cherished gift from his grandmother. She then goes into the bedroom and slams the door. To her, the bowl meant nothing, and John can sweep up the pieces. The crash wakes up Taylor and Kim. They stand speechless in the doorway, drowsy and shaking.

John feels terrible that his precious daughters had to witness Erika's explosive attack. He helps them get into bed and tries to be calm as he carries out their normal bedtime routine. That night, he stretches out on the couch but does not sleep. He knows that there is something very wrong with Erika. Perhaps a move would only worsen her instability. Approaching her mother is the only avenue he knows to try and help her.

Baton Rouge

The next morning, Erika does not come out of the bedroom. John gets the girls ready and takes them to school. He calls Grace and asks her to pick up the girls after school, check on Erika, and maintain the peace. He gets an early flight to Baton Rouge.

The arrangements have been made. Flight 705 will be leaving for Baton Rouge in two hours. John will be on that flight. Overwhelmed and exhausted, he manages to sleep on the plane. After the plane lands, he hails a taxi. The yellow cab drops him off at the modest house of Elizabeth Keppel. When he knocks at the door, a kind elderly woman opens it. He introduces himself and asks if she is Elizabeth Keppel, the mother of Erika Keppel. She confirms that she is. John tells her that he is married to Erika. Tears start rolling down her face as she invites him into the house.

They sit on an old worn couch and John notices right away that she has no tattoos on her arms. The home appears outdated but clean and tidy. She calls to her husband, "Howard, you have to come in here!" He comes into the room and she introduces him as her husband, Erika's father. "Howard, this is John, he is married to our daughter." John reaches out to shake Howard's trembling hand. It appears to John that Howard has turned pale; the older man quickly sits down. The only words he spoke were, "Oh my."

John can hardly believe what he is seeing. He takes a picture of Erika out of his wallet and they say, "Yes, that's our daughter. Is she okay?" John tells them that she is having some emotional problems and he wanted to find out more about her childhood in hopes that he could help her.

They show him pictures of Erika ranging from early childhood to her high school years. As they pull pictures out of a box, they smile. He realizes how much they love her. They explain how their only child began having problems very young and after she graduated from high school, they never saw her again. They told him how she was able to go to college on a golf scholarship and it seemed that she didn't need them anymore. She never contacted them. They had always loved her and prayed that one day she would come back home.

John asked, "What kind of problems did she have as a child?"

They take turns explaining that she was a spiteful and angry child. One Easter, they bought her a baby chick and found her holding it under the water until it died. Howard explains, "When we caught her lying she would cry big tears. We knew they weren't real." Elizabeth says, "It got so we couldn't trust anything she said. It was as if she felt no guilt from the bad things that she did. We think we figured out how she became that person. She would go see movies that were satanic and evil." Erika thrived on scary stories. She and a friend would play with a Ouija board.

John told them about Erika's stories of abuse and they assured him that it was not true. They had been married 42 years and had worked hard to raise their daughter as best they could. Erika refused to attend their small Baptist church and denounced religion entirely from an early age. John thanked and assured them that he would do whatever it took to get help for Erika. He walked out of their home feeling exasperated and thoroughly shocked. He paused for a moment in their yard, overwhelmed with dizziness and nausea. How was he going to live with this? How could such a gorgeous woman have such a temper?

Turning Point

At the airport, John rushes to the gate to get the next flight home. After taking his seat, he calls Mark. Mark and Heidi have wanted to talk to him. John's voice is strained and heavy. He has a lot on his mind. Heidi tells him that Erika admitted to being abusive to Taylor. The news breaks John's heart.

He's back in Mooresville late the same day. Grace has the girls in bed when he gets home. Grace tells him, "Erika hasn't come out of her bedroom once since the girls came home from school. I knocked on her door to ask if she needed anything but there was no reply." Grace notices John's stress level is high and prays with him before leaving.

Erika is in the bedroom and doesn't realize John is home. He's wondering about the strange call from Mark and not quite settled on how to approach his wife. John picks up the phone in the kitchen to call Mark again. Erika and Nancy are talking, he listens and is astounded by what he hears.

"I am sure I can convince John to keep us in this area. We will just cut off all visits with his mother. I'm going to have that new house. John trusts me so he'll listen to me. If we move to Colorado, I will lose all plea-sure of destroying Diane."

Nancy says, "It's amazing how you set her up. From what you've told me, she actually believes she is losing her memory. She deserved everything you did to her."

Erika responds, "That's what she gets for not want-ing John to marry me. John turned against her just like I wanted." John's in shock to hear this—he remains silent and listens.

"I know how much you enjoyed the game. Your strategies worked. John believed it all. You're the best at faking tears and trembling. You make it look so real, it's genius."

"Nancy, it was fun but if John knew how much I despise Taylor and how mean I am to her, he'd be livid!"

Suddenly there is a loud click on the land line, "Nancy, I heard something. Oh no, John's home! I gotta go!" She slams down the phone. Fearing what's next, she cowers like a child. Erika hears him coming up the stairs, each step echoes the terrible pounding in her chest.

John walks in, his face is pale, and he appears to be shaking as he unfolds his rage. "Erika, don't say a word, I heard it all. I loved you with my whole heart, yet you played me and my family. You lied about everything, my mom, her memory and our relationship. You've deeply hurt me; your evil spirited ways hurt my precious Taylor. How could you harm such a sweet little girl? I'm devas-tated! To realize that every doubt I had about my moth-er's memory was planted in my brain by your devilish lips. I can't stand to look at you! I'm aware that hurting my mother was fun for you. My mother's mind is absolutely fine. All because of your wicked antics, I hurt her. You are the epitome of evil!"

Erika is caught in her vindictive game. She tries not to look at John. Tears are running down his face and he is trembling.

Erika screams out, "It's your fault John! You had no right to listen in on my phone call. John snaps back, "Are you blaming me because I learned the truth? Get your stuff and get out. I mean now." John looks at what used to be Erika's beautiful face and suddenly it appears demonic. He believes she must be possessed to do the things she did. He can see evil in her eyes. Suddenly he is afraid of her. She is demon possessed! Shaken and broken, he wants to get away from her.

Erika abruptly turns and heads to her closet. Her body language speaks to how furious she is as she jerks her clothes off the hangers. She dials up Nancy who asks, "How much did he hear?"

"All of it. Now I have to decide where I'll go and what I'll do next. It's over here. How could I have been so careless? I've ruined it. I was so close to having all my dreams come true. I wanted that house, my mansion. I deserved it."

Jacksonville

Nancy has a great idea. "Why don't you go to Jackson-ville? Brian is happily married there. Get even with his mother, now is your chance."

"Great idea. I'll wreak havoc in that marriage, get rid of his mother, and I'll have Brian again. Did I tell you that he's a thoracic surgeon?" I can still get that big house, an estate of my own. He will be able to afford a mansion. It's time to escape from here."

John wishes he could have protected his girls. With Erika out of their lives, he will make it up to them. He knows that Christ is the hope and anchor of his soul. Christ alone will heal them of the evil harm that was done to his family. He was blinded by his love for Erika.

John sees her loading her belongings into the Ascent. He could care less about the car. His life has been turned upside down. He will visit his parents first thing in the morning. He will assure his daughters that everything is going to be better.

John is restless and tired, yet he can't sleep. His eyes are heavy, his heart is broken. All he thinks about is Erika tormenting his mother and Taylor. He blames himself for not listening to his mother's instincts. Time goes slow, he prays off and on. It isn't daylight yet, but he decides to make coffee. Sleep has evaded him; he's drained of all energy. The image of Erika's face turning demonic was frightening. He thanks God that she is gone and continues to pray for God's grace.

Meanwhile, Erika is driving south on interstate 77. When she is just over the South Carolina border, she dials up Nancy again. She doesn't care that it's almost 4 a.m. She needs to talk to her friend and that's all that matters. She's feeling like her old self, no guilt. She's feeling good about another new start, this time in Jacksonville, Florida. The two of them come up with great ideas on how to punish Brian's mother. Sweet revenge! Nancy, with her passive-aggressive personality, gets her kicks by encouraging her. Erika says, "Call me vindictive, call me evil, I will destroy Brian's mother. I'm excited about another challenge. I will have victory next time. She ruined my relationship with her son." The damage she did to John and his family is officially in the past with no hint of remorse on her part.

Nancy laughs, "You will win next time. I know you, Erika. You'll end up with an incredible mansion or die trying. Are you ready to tell me who shot Emil? I'm ready."

Erika admits, "It was me." Nancy responds, "I just wanted to hear you say it."

"You've been on my mind. I was watching a mystery movie when you called."

Suddenly Nancy's ears nearly burst from the sounds of Erika's screams. The shrill screech penetrates her ears, "Oh no, no!" There's an extremely loud noise, the sound of metal crushing and glass breaking.

Nancy cries, "Erika, Erika!" There is no response. The line goes dead. Erika dies instantly. In a fraction of a second she is standing before her judge in heaven, Jesus Christ.

Hours later, the South Carolina state patrol officer finds John's business card with his name and number in Erika's wallet. They contact the North Carolina state patrol. An officer is sent to the home of John Barringer.

John is noticeably distraught when he answers the door. The officer asks John for identification and asks if Erika Barringer is his wife. He confirms she is. She appeared to be talking on the phone while traveling on I-77 southbound when she came upon road construction. Traveling at a high speed she hit an embankment. She did not survive the crash. He asked John to come to the morgue to identify her body. John asks the officer to please wait while he asks his parents to watch his daughters. He feels numb as he goes to the phone to call his parents.

"Dad, please put Mom on speakerphone. Forgive me, I'm so very sorry. Your prayers were answered. Your son and grandchildren are not moving to Colorado. The truth came out. Erika set you up Mom, to make it look like you were mean to her and that you were losing your mind. She was getting even with you for not wanting me to marry her. She was abusive to Taylor and lied to me about her past. I made her leave late last night. I'll talk to you later, but I have some worse news. A state trooper is here now. He came to inform me that Erika was driving on I-77 South this morning when she hit an embankment. She did not survive. Could you come and stay with the girls so I can go to the morgue to identify her body?"

John's parents are filled with grief. Tears fill Diane's eyes as she says, "I am very sad and so sorry for Erika. I wish she could have known the Lord. She heard the gospel many times in church, but her heart was hardened. Her life was cut short; all lives are short when we consider eternity."

Somehow, John knew that God was speaking to him through all of this. He had deeply loved Erika and regretted that she was a lost soul. Her body may be in the morgue, but her soul has been in the 'life there after' for hours, ever since she drew her last breath.

Meanwhile, back in Albany, NY, Nancy has called the South Carolina State Patrol. Farcus is a broken person. She can't endure the pain, her best friend is dead. Erika was her life. Nancy was her confidant and soulmate. Recovery will be long and painful, if at all. She always knew in her heart Erika shot Emil, but nothing matters now.

Eternity

In heaven, God sits on His throne, high and lifted up. His robe fills the temple. (Isaiah 6:1–3) The seraphim call out "Holy, Holy, Holy. Heaven and earth are full of His glory." Erika now knows God the Savior is real. He is now her judge.

Erika is overwrought with the shocking revelation of knowing that her life on earth is over, she is now entering eternity. She is flooded with the remembrance of every sin she committed and those she had forgotten. She also recalls every sermon she ever heard.

Suddenly she's aware that she will miss the indescribable gift that God has prepared for those whose name is written in the Book of Life. She remembers the preacher quoting the scripture: "In My Father's house are many mansions. I go to prepare a place for you. That where I am ye may be also." (John 14:2–3)

Again, she doesn't get the mansion, she's furious! Mansions in heaven are too glorious to comprehend. She now knows it's all real, but a heavenly mansion is not in Erika's future. In the presence of God, she falls prostrate, paralyzed with fear and trepidation. She is unable to lift her head. Erika cries out, "If I could have my life back, I would worship God." She begs for forgiveness but it's too late. Her fate is sealed. Suddenly she gets a glimpse of Jennifer Davis entering a mansion. She tells herself, "It must be a mirage. Jennifer couldn't afford one of those." When Erika realizes they are rent-free forever, it boggles her mind. She cries out, "I could have had one." She is still thinking of herself.

An angel appears and says, "Erika, I cannot find your name in the Lamb's Book of Life."

Instantaneously she is swept into a fearful tunnel and is uncannily aware that this place was waiting for her. There are countless, gruesome, disfigured demons hovering around her. They are hissing; their green eyes dart without focusing. The smell is repugnant, burning her nostrils. Her body is eternal, it can never die again. Excruciating pain will be everlasting. She now realizes that no sinful pleasure was worth the agony of going to hell. It is the second death.

Next, as she advances down the semi-dark tunnel, she sees a bright light. She recalls one sermon she heard. "Satan can transform himself into an angel of light." (II Corinthians 11:14). Erika is aware, she's moving toward a large lake of flames. She never believed in the rebirth that Christ offers. Now the second death is clearly seen.

Born twice, die once,

Born once, die twice.

She hears a scream. A newcomer trips on a man begging for a drop of water to cool his tongue. (Luke 16:24) She is shocked to see Marty Scott moving helplessly within the tunnel. "Why are you here Marty? You weren't evil, you even taught Sunday School."

"That's right, but I never asked for God's forgiveness. I never prayed for Christ's blood on the cross to cover my sins. I did plan to, but a surprise heart attack got me first. I felt young and bullet proof. My regrets are many, but regrets are worthless."

Marty and Erika disappear into the gloom, never to cross paths again. They are entering hell where time is never measured again. No need for calendars or clocks, eternity is forever. There's no exit, just an entrance. Erika wishes she could warn Nancy to search for the truth.

Further down the tunnel, she's stunned to see a man that looks familiar. "Is that you Emil? Why are you here? You went to confession at your church every morning."

"Yes I did, but no one ever told me only Jesus Christ can forgive sins. I was betrayed by my church. No one ever told me that it is a sin to pray to anyone other than the Trinity: God the Father, Jesus the Son, and the Holy Spirit." (Matthew 28:19). God will not share His glory. "I am the Lord: that is my name: and my glory I will not give to another, neither my praise to a graven image." (Isaiah 42:8) They pray to a false god that cannot save. (Isaiah 45:20)

John Remarries

Twelve years have passed. It's a cool fall morning in North Carolina, a wonderful time of year. The hot summer is gone, days are shorter. John has built a fire in the fireplace to take the chill out of the air. He sits down with a cup of coffee and the Bible open on his lap. He loves these early mornings, before his wife gets up, when he can meditate on God and His precious Son. He reflects on his life and how good God has been to him. He is blessed to have a strong Christian mother whose kindness and forgiveness means a lot to him. He is thankful for His wife, Julie, a missionary's daughter, and their 10 years of marriage. He rejoices and praises God for his daughters who love and serve God. He bows his head and gives thanks. Taylor and Kim are now teenagers and thinking about what college they'll attend. CoCo, their faithful dog, a gift from Mark and Heidi twelve years ago, is curled up napping at his feet. It's a happy Christian family. All the bad memories have faded.

Each morning it's his wife's routine to tune into the morning worship hour. "The Love of God" is softly playing as Julie reminds him, "Remember, we've invited your parents over for breakfast today. Taylor and Kim are already at the door welcoming them in." The song continues to play as they gather to enjoy Julie's delicious quiche. This is a family united and Christ centered.

Buy at Amazon.com Share on Facebook, Instagram, Twitter, Parler, Rumble and Mewe

"Daughter-in-Law from Hell" was
first written as a screen play.

Please send comments about the book to:
Leigh Williams
P.O. Box 903
Davidson, NC 28036

Don't let Satan prevent you from spending eternity with God.

Fall on your knees, repent. Don't let a sin you love prevent you from a forever home with God.

Trustworthy Web Sites

Adrianrogers.com
Johnmccarther.com
FindingTruePeace.com

To purchase a highly regarded hard cover Bible with accurate footnotes, order the Study Bible from Institute of Creation Research.

Order line 800-628-7640
Excellent choice for those searching
Find a solid Christian radio ministry

- BBN Bible Broadcast Network
- Read Erwin Lutzer's books (author and pastor— Moody Bible Institute, Chicago)
- Moody Broadcasting Chicago, Cleveland, Meadville, Pa. or MoodyRadio.org
- Find a good Bible-based church. Read the Bible so you'll be able to detect false teaching. It isn't just about love, although **God does love us**. He cannot look on sin; He's Holy and righteous. God warns us of what sin is. He clearly lays it out. The following verses show what God is

against. Being obedient to Christ is our goal and our only hope for heaven.

- Read 50 Years in the Church of Rome by Charles Chiniquay. Buy it on Amazon.

Verses From King James Bible

Peter 5:8

Satan is like a roaring lion walking about, looking for who he can destroy.

John 3:16

For God so loved the world the He gave His only begotten Son, that whosoever believeth in him should not perish, but have everlasting life.

Amos 8:11–12 (Jewish Nation)

Behold the days come, saith the Lord God, that I will send a famine in the land, not a famine of bread nor of thirst for water, but of hearing the words of the Lord. (Refers to Israel.)

And they shall wander from sea to sea and from the north even to the east, they shall run to and fro to seek the word of the Lord and shall not find it. (Refers to Israel)

Amos 9:15

And I will plant them upon their land, and they shall no more be pulled out of their land which I have given them, saith the Lord thy God. (God returns Israel's land)

Acts 28:24

And some believed the things which were spoken, and some believed not.

John 3:15–17

For God so loved the world, that he gave his only begotten Son, that whosoever believeth in Him shall not perish, but have everlasting life. (Jesus is the son of God. Jesus is God because the trinity is all three in one)

Revelation 19:16

And he hath on His vesture and on His thigh a name written, King of

Kings, and Lord of Lords. (refers to Jesus Christ)

John 14:2

In my father's house are many mansions: if it were not so I would have told you. I go to prepare a place for you.

Revelation 21:27

And they shall in no wise enter into it any thing that defileth, neither whatsoever worketh abomination, or maketh a lie: but they which are written in the Lamb's book of life. (Is your name written in the Lamb Book of Life?)

Isaiah 44:15–17

Man maketh graven idols and falls down to worship them. (God calls this sin.)

Isaiah 45:5

I am the Lord, and there is none else, there is no God beside me.

I Timothy 2:5

> For there is one God, and <u>one</u> <u>mediator</u> between God and men, the man Christ Jesus.
> God's anger was poured against the people that worshipped the queen of heaven and other gods. (Read Jeremiah 7:18–28)

Matthew 28:19

> Go ye therefore, and teach all nations, baptizing them in the name of the Father, and of the son and of the Holy Ghost. (Trinity)

Hebrews 9:27

> It is appointed unto men once to die, but after this the judgment. (There's no purgatory. Pope Gregory came up with the plan to bring more money into the Catholic Church.)

John 8:58

> Jesus said unto them, Verily, verily I say unto you. Before Abraham was, I am. (Jesus existed before the manger.)

Revelation 1:8

I am Alpha and Omega, the beginning and the ending, saith the Lord. (Jesus existed before the manger. Mary was his earthly mom.)

II Peter 3:9

The Lord is not willing that any should perish, but all come to repentance.

Matthew 7:23

Then will I profess unto them, I never knew you, depart from me. (refers to unsaved or non-Christians)

Revelation 3:5

He that overcometh, the same shall be clothed in white raiment, and I will not blot out his name out of this book of life, but I will confess his name before my Father, and his angels.

Ephesians 2:20

Jesus Christ himself being the chief corner stone. (not Peter)

Colossians 1:14–20

In whom we have redemption through His blood, even the forgiveness of sins. Who is the image of the invisible God, the first born of every creature.

For by Him were all things created, that are in heaven, and that are in earth, visible and invisible, whether they be thrones, or dominions, or principalities, or powers: All things were created by Him and for Him.

And he is before all things, and by Him all things consist. (Jesus Christ)

I Corinthians 1:18

For the preaching of the cross is to them that perish foolishness, but unto us which are saved it is the power of God.

Matthew 7:14

Strait is the gate and narrow is the way, which leadeth life, and few there be that find it.

Beware of false prophets, which come to you in sheep's clothing, but inwardly are ravening wolves.

Hebrews 2:3

How shall we escape, if we neglect so great a salvation?

Isaiah 64:6

All our righteousnesses are as filthy rags; we all do fade as a leaf. (Nothing you do can save you, it's worthless. Jesus paid it all. Accept it, it's a free gift.)

Psalms 14:1

The fool hath said in his heart, there is no God. They are corrupt, they have done abominable works, there is none the doeth good.

Luke 16: 23–24

And in hell he lifts up his eyes, being in torments, and seeth Abraham afar off, and Lazarus in his bosom.

And he cried and said, Father Abraham, have mercy on me, and send Lazarus, that he may dip his finger in water and cool my tongue, for I am tormented in this flame.

Joshua 24: 15–16

> But as for me and my house, we will serve the Lord. God forbid that we should forsake the Lord, to serve other gods.

Isaiah 7:14

> Behold a virgin shall conceive and bear a son, and shall call His name Immanuel.

Isaiah 5:20

> Woe to him that call evil good and good evil.
> Sins God Hates (Look up these verses in your Bible)

Revelation 21:7–8

1 Corinthians 6:9–10

Galations 5: 19–21

Read Matthew 24

This prophecy tells the signs of the end. God will some day put an end to this world. (No one knows the day.) We are to look for signs.

Nation shall war against nation.

1. False religions will increase.
2. Famines and pestilences will increase (deadly disease).
3. Earthquakes will increase.
4. Christians will be hated as Jesus was hated.
5. The Gospel will have been preached worldwide...and then the end will come.
6. God will make all things new.

Credits

Books

Seuss, Dr. Theodor. *Green Eggs and Ham*. New York. Random House. 1960.
Willems, Mo. *Don't Let the Pigeon Drive the Bus*. New York. Disney Hyperion. 2003.

Game

Hasbro, *Candyland*. Eleanor Abbott 1949

Painting

Verhas, Jan C. *The Broken Pot*. 1876. (Bruce Museum), Greenwich

Music

Title	Composed By	Sung By
Born Free	John Barry Don Black	Matt Monro
Grandma Got Run Over By a Reindeer	Randy Brooks	Elmo and Patsy Shropshire
Wonderful Tonight	Eric Clapton	Eric Clapton

The Way You Look Tonight	Dorothy Fields Jerome Kern	Frank Sinatra
I'll Be Home For Christmas	Kim Gannon Walter Kent	Bing Crosby
Fly Me to the Moon	Bart Howard	Frank Sinatra Count Basie
At Last	Mack Gordon Harry Warren	Etta James
Yellow Rose of Texas	Edwin Pearce Christy JK 1853	Mitch Miller
The Love of God	Frederick Lehman Claudia Mays	Mercyme Gaithers
Can't Help Falling in Love	Hugo Peretti Luigi Creature George Weiss	Elvis Presley
Bridal Chorus	Richard Wagner	Metropolitan Opera Orchestra of Lohengrin
For Once in My Life	Ron Miller Orlando Murden	Stevie Wonder

About the Author

This well-travelled author was graduated from a Christian college with a Bachelor of Science degree. She taught in public schools until becoming an entrepreneur, designing for a nationally known company while starting her own business. Department stores sold her designs in the baby department as well as the home décor department. She was also featured in three national magazines. Recently becoming an author of fiction, she is using this new avenue to release her creativity. But most of all, to make known the truth of God's wonderful plan of salvation.

CPSIA information can be obtained
at www.ICGtesting.com
Printed in the USA
LVHW080827270321
682666LV00033B/1200